I0746079

SCARRED

Mia Kerick

A NineStar Press Publication

Published by NineStar Press
P.O. Box 91792,
Albuquerque, New Mexico, 87199 USA.
www.ninestarpress.com

Scarred

Copyright © 2018 by Mia Kerick
Cover Art by Natasha Snow Copyright © 2018
Edited by Elizabetta McKay

This is a work of fiction. Names, characters, places, and incidents are either the product of the author's imagination or are used fictitiously. Any resemblance to actual persons living or dead, business establishments, events, or locales is entirely coincidental.

All rights reserved. No part of this publication may be reproduced in any material form, whether by printing, photocopying, scanning or otherwise without the written permission of the publisher. To request permission and all other inquiries, contact NineStar Press at the physical or web addresses above or at Contact@ninestarpress.com.

Printed in the USA
First Edition
December, 2018

Print ISBN: 978-1-949909-78-4

Also available in eBook, ISBN: 978-1-949909-76-0

Warning: This book contains sexually explicit content, which is only suitable for mature readers, child abduction, the graphic discussion and depiction of sexual abuse of a child, PTSD symptoms, and a homophobic beating/ gay bashing.

Even in paradise, beautiful faces can hide scarred souls.

ONE tropical island.

Placida Island's gentle ocean breezes and rolling surf beckon to those who wish to reside in remote tropical serenity.

TWO men living in self-imposed exile.

Wearing twisted ropes of mutilated skin on his back and carrying devastating damage in his soul from severe childhood abuse, Matthew North lives alone in a rustic cabin on the shore, avoiding human contact.

Gender fluidity his perceived "crime" against family and friends, Vedie Wilson flees his childhood home so he can freely express his identity.

THREE persecutors seeking their warped view of justice.

Vedie's past refuses to stay in the faraway city he left behind when family members, intent on forcing him to change, threaten the precious peace he's found.

TOO MANY scars to count.

Their beautiful faces masking deeply scarred souls, Matt and Vedie live in hiding from the world and each other.

Can they unite and embrace each other's painful pasts, leaving the scars behind, to find love?

2015

Chapter One

VEDIE

By ten, I'm sweaty as a deckhand from bussing tables on the beach, and I'm sorely in need of a brew or six. But seeing as I've got no cash to burn, I'm gonna have to leave my coworkers—who're revving up over by the tiki bar—to their night of hard partying. I grab my leopard-print backpack from the hook on the back wall of the bar and head to the men's room to turn into the other me.

And just as I figured, Joey's waiting on me there. "You gonna come party with us tonight, sweet Vedie?"

"No can do, Joey, much as I want to." Safe inside a stall, I pull off my sweaty green The Only Tiki Hut on Placida Island work T-shirt. As soon as I replace it with a dark red, stretchy lace off-the-shoulder number, I can breathe easy. Next, I strip off my khaki shorts and yank on my favorite black velvet pair. Even though I've gotta ride my bike home, I kick my high-tops into my backpack and slide on a pair of jeweled flip-flops. After taking a quick piss, I head out of the stall and plant my ass in front of the mirror beside Joey, who's standing there like he's got nothing better to do than count the drips of water leaking from the faucet.

"Lookin' good, pretty Miss Vedie...mmmhmm..."

No matter if I'm dressed like a dude or a lady, Joey always stares at me like I'm a juicy bowl of strawberry shortcake—he licks his lips, and I know he wants to take himself a nice big bite of a flavor he can't get at home. Then he slaps his hand hard against my thigh, and creepy-slow, it climbs my leg. It's headed for my ass cheek, or my name ain't Vedie Wilson.

"Hands out of the cookie jar, Joey, my man." I don't appreciate it when any dude gropes me without asking for permission first. But the sad truth is I'm never gonna want *Joey's* hands on me. While he gawks, I pull a shimmery hairband out of my bag and wrap it around my head to hold the damp dreads off my face. "Got yourself a sweet tooth, looks like, Joey. You'd be wise to get your ass home to your sweet wife, not that you asked me for no words of wisdom."

"Not gonna even think about goin' home 'til I had me some fun," Joey replies, jamming his hand in his pocket— probably to keep it from curving around my ass.

When I bend to rinse the sweat off my face, he stays quiet and doesn't goose me. Maybe this time he heard what I told him about getting his ass home to Mrs. Joey. But more likely he's checking out my butt.

"Baybeee...uh-huh...mmmhmm...nice ass you got there in them sweet little shorts..."

I sigh real loud, "I've got some shit to do here, big dawg, so if that's all you wanted." The only way to get this guy to take a hike is to tell him point-blank that he's gotta head on out. "Catch ya on the flip side."

He leans in so close his scratchy beard brushes my neck, and I shiver in the bad way. He takes a deep sniff—I guess he likes the smell of sweaty dude—and then finally bails. And right about now, I sorely wish the tiki hut restaurant had one of those one-person anything goes restrooms—for a dude, a lady, or whoever you feel like at the moment—but at least now I'm finally alone in the men's room.

I pull out my makeup bag and quickly powder my nose so it doesn't shine in the moonlight, and I glide a deep shade of maroon over my lips. But I take the time to be an artist with my eyeliner and mascara because I figure eyes oughta say something. When I look good enough that *I'd* wanna do me if I got hot for ladies, I figure I'm looking good enough for public viewing. And my new perfume smells like the freedom I've got down here on Placida Island—coconuts and wildflowers and the ocean and honey. I spray it on heavy all over my neck and chest.

As I saunter out of the men's room, I don't miss that it's funny how I went in here looking all-dude, but coming out, you could mistake me for a lady. *Ha!* More like a red-hot, sexy mama—smooth and silky everywhere except for the four-day beard.

I'm a guy, though, even when I'm dressed this fine. And in my opinion—not that anybody gives two shits what I think—the combo of smooth legs and a stubbly chin says, *in your face, assholes!* I don't have to choose how I show myself to the world anymore.

"HOT DAMN! WHO be dat fine lady?" Joey knows I'm no lady, and I wish he'd shut his trap. I turn my head away and roll my eyes twice as I head past the bar. "Who's the lucky guy who's gonna get some of dat tonight?"

"Not gonna be you, Joey." And sure, I say it out loud, but not loud enough for him to hear, because I don't want to piss him off. Pissed-off dudes can be dangerous.

I've only been working here a week-and-a-day now, but I'm pretty sure my coworkers are cool with how I dress. At work, I have to wear my green Tiki Hut T-shirt and tan shorts, just like everybody else. But I don't hide my ladylike side down here on Placida Island; I'm never gonna hide her again. The world thinks the way I show myself is all fucked-up, but I've come to understand that it is what it is, and it's why I'm never going back to Boston. I can't go back up there and be me—not if I want to live to see another day.

"Haven't you people ever seen a boy dressed up nice and pretty before?" I shout it back over my shoulder, flashing a big grin, knowing my lips look good, all shiny and red.

"Vedie, have yourself a good evening!" one of the ladies calls out. I smile inside because I think some of my coworkers like the *real* me, and I'm not used to being liked just the way I am. Maybe the rule truly is "anything goes" on this tropical island in the middle of nowhere.

I glance around to see if Crazy Matt is lurking around the bar. Crazy Matt—that's the name all of the waiters at The Only Tiki Hut gave to this gorgeous but pissed-off-looking customer I made a play for earlier tonight. I actually leaned down and whispered into his ear, "Take me home tonight, Mateo." I like how Mateo sounds way better than Crazy Matt, and it's pretty much the same damn name, at least it is in my neck of the woods.

I didn't stop and wait for his answer because I know it doesn't work that way with guys like him. If Mateo wants to hook up with me, he'll make it happen. If he doesn't, there's nothing on God's green earth I can do to make him change his mind. So I pointed out real clear that I was one of his options, and then I moved on.

I TOSS A piece of gum in my mouth and head out to the back of the restaurant so I can grab my bike. Picked up an old BMX at a pawn shop as soon as I landed down here on Placida Island, and it's been my set of wheels ever since. It's pretty as a picture—lime-green and white. Soon as I get some extra cash, I'm gonna pick up a hot-pink bike seat. Bonus on the bicycle situation: pumping this baby around the island keeps my ass nice and tight.

I bend over to unlock it, glad that Joey's not around to feel up my ass, because sure as shit, it's what he'd do. I toss the chain into my pack and swing it onto my shoulder thinking I'm looking too fine tonight to head straight home—a total waste of hotness—but, oh well, that's the way it goes when you're broke.

"Hey."

It's funny, but with just this one-word greeting, I recognize the voice.

Chapter Two

VEDIE

Mateo stands in the dark shadows close to the building and somehow looks hot, not creepy.

"Mateo, why're you here?" I don't sound too friendly, but then, me and him aren't friends.

"Guess I'm in the mood for dessert."

The dude's studying me like he's never seen a boy dressed in girl's clothes. When he's done gawking, he tilts his head and asks in a cool voice, "You in drag tonight?"

"Nah. I'm not in drag." I stare him in the eye and add, "This is just how I feel right now." And I wait to see if me being dressed like a lady might be a deal breaker.

He's checking me out, but his eyes are spooked, just like they were when I brought him his first drink at the Tiki Hut. I've seen eyes like his before—right off the bat, they make me think of Mrs. Diaz, my downstairs neighbor back when I was in middle school. She had the exact same look in her eyes on the day of the drive-by shooting near Ryan Playground...the day her little Rosita got shot in the back of the neck.

It's nighttime, so I can't tell if his eyes are dark or light, but they're as hollow as an empty cardboard box dumped on a city sidewalk. And it's like there should be blood smeared on his chin or sprayed across his forehead, because the look on his face screams, "I got jumped!" But there's no blood and no city sidewalk and no Mrs. Diaz hollering in the alley and no shiny black car peeling away with a screech. I can't see anything around us except for the pretty tropical, nighttime sky and palm trees blowing gentle in the breeze—the shit I came down here to no-man's-land for.

I'm lying… That shit's nice, but it's not why I came here.

Warm sun and clear skies dotted with tall palm trees and smiling vacation faces—all fine in my book—aren't the true reasons I went south. The real deal is I'm here to get away from up there. And I'd bet my sorry life that handsome, broken Mateo here, with his "I've been through hell" eyes, came to Placida Island for the same damn reason.

His white ass is hiding—same as my black one is.

Anyhow, I don't look away while he's thinking me over, and when he finally nods, I figure he gets it. Or he kind of gets it, because who the hell really gets shit like Vedie Wilson being a dude who likes to dress like a lady?

"You got a bike?" I'm an official shit-for-brains. Of course the dude didn't come here on a freaking bicycle.

"I've got a truck." He turns around and looks toward a dark-colored pickup in the corner of the parking lot. Not a pimped-out rig with fancy-ass tires, just plain and clean.

"Cool." If we're gonna hook up tonight, I have to go in his truck. There's no way his ass would fit on the back of *my* wheels.

"Let me grab your bike and stick it on the truck bed." He steps forward, looks at my bike for a second—I swear he shudders—and then makes a move to grab it.

But I stop him, remembering in the nick of time not to touch him because the dude might snap my hand off. "No, man. I got it."

He steps right up close. He's tall, way taller than me, even though I've been called a tall glass of water a time or two. And the man smells good—I *so* hope not better than me. "I'll get your bike...you look...well, I-I don't want you to get your outfit messed up."

Heat rushes to my face as quick as tears flood my eyes. I'm not exactly a princess waiting on some knight in shining armor to do my bidding, and his politeness wrecks me. I blink and blink until I've blinked all the wetness away, and of course, I say another something totally dumbass. "Gonna get a hot-pink bike seat one of these days."

Shit. For. Brains.

He grabs my bike and tosses it onto one of his big shoulders, and I follow him across the parking lot to his truck, thinking that if you'd asked me an hour ago, I'd never have figured this sweet shit would be going down between us. I watch as he places my wheels real careful in the truck bed, but when he comes to the passenger side, unlocks the truck, and opens the door for me like a gentleman...I lose it for real.

MATT

Seeing this kid cry slices easily through my thick skin, and I don't appreciate it one bit. There's a heart somewhere under all the armor I wear, but I like to keep it under wraps. What's most fucked-up about this situation, though, is that less than two hours ago, we were complete strangers, not exactly enjoying a friendly interaction.

When he came to my table, he asked, "Yo, man. What're you drinking?" I guess I must have looked at him cross-eyed because I didn't recognize the kid as a regular worker at the Tiki Hut. And I should know; I've eaten dinner here several nights a week for the past decade. But he got right on my case. "What's your friggin' problem? I asked you real nice, seeing as it's my job and shit!"

It was as if he'd read my mind when he sized up my expression, which made me shiver because nobody knows what I'm thinking, and I like it that way.

"Just water," I told him, and then I stared out over the beach, craning my neck like I was watching for somebody even though there's never been anyone for me to watch for.

He hadn't liked being ignored, so he started to play the smart-ass, a part he's quite good at. "Sorry, big dawg, your lady's a no-show. You're gonna have to fill your bed with somebody new tonight, looks like." He'd actually waggled his eyebrows.

"Guess today's not my lucky day because I'm planning to sleep alone," I told him and meant it.

"It *can* be your lucky day if you play your cards right." He let go of the tray with one hand, dropped his palm onto my shoulder, and squeezed. "You don't have to be lonely tonight if you don't—what the fuck, man!"

I'd already jumped to my feet and practically stomped on the guy. "Hands off, asshole."

"I hear you, big dawg, so chill." The kid pulled back his hand and released a long sigh, like he knew he'd broken one of his own rules by grabbing me. "I'll get my dumbass hand off of your badass shoulder, if you sit your ass back down on that chair and chill." And after another sigh, he said, "Not gonna push the issue, man... Just offering you some company on a long, hot, lonely night." Then he'd turned so fast his short dreads flew, and as he walked away, he grumbled, "If I wanted to get slammed for being a faggot I'd go right back up north where I came from."

This is the brief and stormy history of our relationship. And so, with regard to the boy standing before me now, looking damned cute in a lacy shirt and short-shorts, I'm still in full-out fuck-you mode. Nonetheless, I'm here, hoping to take him home for the very same reason. But this sobbing dude in girl's clothes is the polar opposite of the wiseass I met in the restaurant.

Once again, my mind is drawn to what passed between us in the bar. When he'd returned to my table, he told me off quite effectively. "Here you go, sweetness," he delivered this line with a Mona Lisa smile and placed a glass of ice water on the table in front of me. He looked so smug—I wondered if he'd spat into it. "And with this water, my job here is done. Your waiter tonight's gonna be Sheila. I'll be sure to mention to her that you're a friendly sort of dude, who enjoys a nice shoulder massage while placing your order."

"Sheila knows me."

"Then she knows she oughta put on body armor if she plans on brushing your shoulder with her elbow?"

For the record, I try not to ever look anybody directly in the eyes. There's no reason for it. I live alone and work online, with four cats to keep me company, and besides that, I always have someone to talk to because I talk to *myself* all day, every day. But I glared right into his light eyes and informed him, "She already knows how I am."

Then the guy grinned.

And for some crazy reason, I smiled back.

God knows I didn't want to smile. In fact, it'd been so long since my lips formed the unfamiliar shape, I was afraid they'd get stuck that way and never go back to the straight line I always wear. I wouldn't be able to scare off the whole damned world while wearing a stupid, shit-eating grin, now, would I?

But our unexpected grins had opened a door, and when he said, "Keep this in mind, Mister So-sha-bull—my offer still stands. If you decide you want something sweet and warm and chocolaty brown for dessert, I get off work at ten." I took him at his word, so here I am.

But he's not smiling right now. "Listen...uh..."

"My name's Vedie...and I ain't crying." It takes him five deep breaths to make sure of this.

"Yeah...um, Vedie, if you want to come to my place with me, you know, it would be good. But if you want me to drive you home, that'd be fine, too." My pick-up line isn't smooth. In my defense, I'm extremely rusty in this department. Still, I hold open the car door and wait for him to slide his ass onto the leather seat.

The kid wipes his nose with a stretchy lace sleeve and shakes his head. "Don't wanna go home, Mateo."

I make a quick decision, because if he's coming with me, he's going to need to calm down. I don't do well with drama. So I reach past him to the center console, grab a tissue, and tell him in a firm voice, "Dry off your face."

He takes the tissue and dabs at his eyes. "My mascara's probably all over the place by now."

I glance at his face and shake my head. "No. You still look good."

"Mama always told me honesty is the very best policy, though it didn't do me too much good when I tried to explain to her that sometimes I get into dressing like a girl."

What on earth is Vedie trying to get across by filling me in on his mother's favorite saying? I'm tempted to pinch myself to make sure I'm awake, because I could very well be dreaming up this whole warped scene.

"And all I'm gonna say, Mateo, is you treated me...*different* from what I'm used to...and on account of that, I lost it."

I stand beside him, nodding like I understand what he's trying to tell me.

"So give me a minute to grab my bike from your truck, and I'll get outta your hair. We can pretend like this shit never went down."

And this is when I break my brand-new rule regarding interacting with hot young men dressed like ladies in dark parking lots. I reach out and touch him. I don't grab him; I just brush his arm with my fingertips. "No, Vedie. I want you to come back to my place."

He doesn't even have to think it over. "I can do that." Vedie speaks brightly and slides his ass onto my passenger seat. I push the door closed, go around the car, and hop in, my head spinning with this strange turn of events.

In silence, I pull my truck out of the parking lot and head south, down the coast. We both open up our windows and lean back, letting the wind blow away our worries. Or it's what I'm trying to do, but I can't stop my lips from moving as I silently verbalize the raging thoughts in my head.

ONCE WE'RE ON the screened porch, Vedie bends to look through the window into my kitchen. "You've got a lot of cats," he says in a soft voice.

My cats are sitting in a crooked line—on the floor, the table, the chair, and the windowsill—staring out at us with calculating eyes.

"I only have four."

My first-ever houseguest places all ten of his long, delicate fingers lightly on the screen. Jennifer, the oldest female, a fluffy tiger, presses her nose against them, one by one.

"They're waiting on you," he says. "I love cats, you know. I had a few...back home." He sniffs and wipes his nose again.

I hope this means he's finished with the crying. And I don't ask him where "back home" is because it doesn't matter. I already know tonight is a big mistake. But like the lonely fool I am, I unlock the door, hold it wide, and allow my eyes to follow along as he enters *my* home. Since the day almost a decade ago when I bought this cottage, he is the only human being besides my parents and me who has ever walked through these doors. And he'll soon discover that the fluffy creatures are the only decorations I keep. "The cats aren't used to people."

"What are their names?"

I'm going to check out soon. I always do. The instant anybody starts asking me personal questions is when it happens, and it happens every time. No exceptions. The mental rug is always ripped out from beneath my brain.

I may be crazy, but at least I'm consistent.

"They've got names, don't they?" He kneels on the floor, careful to keep his knees together.

"The one you're petting is named Jen...Jennifer." Ugh... TMI. I suddenly feel vulnerable.

So I focus on the details of my first-ever houseguest— his face, his hair, his skin. I'd say he's not bad looking, if shit like that mattered to me. But shit like handsome or hot or sexy is immaterial to the forward progression of my life. Never made a difference to me, never will. If it did make a difference, I'd admit Vedie's skin looks inviting—the color of the steaming sand on the beach in front of my cottage in the late afternoon right after a rainstorm. A sassy boy-man with a face of constantly changing expressions—full lips that twist and turn and eyes too light to be natural, his expression amused and teasing and a little bit smart-assed.

And then there's his hair—you don't see hair like his every day. Sticking out right and left—tangled stubby dreadlock frizz. Back at the bar, the sight of it had made me want to laugh, and not just a silent snicker inside my head.

I wanted to laugh out loud—I wanted to laugh for real. But right now, it doesn't look comical like it did in the restaurant. It looks crazy and disheveled and wild, much like I feel.

And there's something timid in the light aqua-green eyes that don't seem to belong in his dark-skinned face, watchful and wary like those of the deer that feed on the apples I toss into my backyard every morning. They want the damn apples, and they'll risk about anything to get them, but they're bloody terrified. So, yeah, everything I'd need to know about this man is written in those easy-to-read eyes.

He breaks into a huge grin, and it hits me: I don't think I could be afraid of this young man if I tried. "Jennifer? You named your kitty Jennifer?"

He doesn't need to know I named her after Jennifer Aniston, whose character on *Friends* reruns is so warm and likable. "And the one sitting on the chair is named Charlie." On *Two and a Half Men* reruns, Charlie Sheen seems like a fun guy to have around. No commitment necessary with him—a drive-by friend, which works well for me.

He reaches up to pet my big black cat. "Hi, Charlie..." After sniffing his hand, Charlie lets Vedie scratch his neck. "Look, Mateo—he's letting me scratch him. I think he likes me." And I think Vedie's enjoying the scratching session almost as much as Charlie is. "What are them two's names?" He glances to the windowsill at the two younger cats.

"The orange one is Conan." I wonder if he's detected a too-much-television-watching pattern in the themes of my cats' names. "And the gray one, he's Bob." It's Sponge Bob, to be exact, but I don't feel a need to confess all of the tiny details to a man who, after tonight, I will likely only see in passing at the Tiki Bar. But the sad truth is, other than these cats, TV is my only companion.

"You gave your cats people names."

"Uh-huh." I walk over to the refrigerator. "Care for a beer...or a soda?"

"I'll take a brew. Long night at work...and hot, too."

I can't believe I'm still here with this guy. Mentally, I mean. I guess I'm just a little bit too lonely—as desperate for human contact as a man shipwrecked on a tropical island for ten years—because I'm not sure I'm gay, and I'm definitely not into whatever it is this guy, who's decked out in lace and velvet and wearing full makeup on top of his scruffy beard, is into. But still, I'm doing this.

"Come on, let's go to the couch. You must be ready to get off your feet." It sounds like I want him on his back, and that thought makes my dick go numb. "What I mean is, we can sit and talk, I guess."

Vedie rises to his feet in a ladylike manner and flashes a smile, followed by a little bit of eyelash batting, as if he's trying to flirt. With me. Crazy Matt. "Cool. I could sit for a few."

I head to the living room followed by Vedie, Jennifer, and finally, Charlie, all in a row, like I'm the Pied Fucking Piper. Before we even get to the simple brown couch, Conan and Sponge Bob go racing by all of us. My cats are apparently far more comfortable with having company than I am, but I'm still here. I'm still here.

I gesture to the couch, and Vedie sits and crosses his legs. I take a seat beside him, if you count two feet away to be "beside" somebody. And I'm expecting it to happen. Any second now, my head's going to jump ship, leaving only my body bobbing aimlessly on the open water.

Looks like I'm needy enough for a little physical contact that I'm willing to give this a shot. And there's always an outside chance I'll stick around for the good stuff.

Strangely, the change happens in Vedie, not me. He sits up straight and his shoulders go back and the word sassy again pops into my racing brain. "So you don't have any questions for me?"

I'm surprised by his boldness. His eyes flash in a way that makes my consciousness briefly dim, and I ask, "Uh...questions?"

"About all of this?" He gestures to his outfit, and then he actually pulls off one of his decorative sandals and holds it high in the air. I think he might swat me with it, but he relaxes his fingers and drops it to the floor. "And the makeup and stuff." As soon as he utters the words "makeup," he seems to remember the damage his crying episode likely did to his mascara. He pulls a polka-dotted zipper bag out of his leopard-print backpack and retrieves a small powder compact, which he pops open to carefully fix his eyes.

"Not my business, I guess."

"Not your business?" He stuffs the bag of cosmetics back into his pack. "Big dawg, I'm in your house, on your couch, drinking your beer. And um...aren't we gonna...you know...get busy tonight?"

This is when it happens. The numbness starts in my belly and quickly spreads north to my head and south to my toes, and just like that, I'm a mere bystander in my own living room, watching the hazy events from above.

VEDIE

"Mateo...hey, man, you okay?"

I'm not about to pretend like I'm some kind of head doctor, but something major is wrong with this dude. I try and push away the warped realization that this makes two big-time fucked-up people in one small, plain-ass cottage. I oughta be thinking that I'm so out of here because this dude is wack. And besides, seeing as he hasn't got any pretty curtains on his windows, we can't have a single thing in common. But I'm not leaving. Because I just saw the light leave a man's eyes—like the light went out of little Rosita's eyes, right there on the sidewalk that July day so long ago. The thing is, this guy hasn't been shot, and he's still breathing, far as I can tell, and...and I'm no Mother Teresa, but this guy needs serious help.

I'm hesitant to touch the dude seeing as he nearly offed me last time I tried, but I figure it's a chance I have to take. "I'm gonna put my hands on you, man, but I'm not gonna hurt you, and I ain't gonna try and mess with you, either. Got me? I'm gonna lie beside you on this here couch and hold onto you. Ya got me?"

No response from the guy, but I don't let that stop me, probably because I'm a dumbass. I somehow manage to pull him down and lean sideways on the end of the couch, with Mateo hunkered down real awkward beside me.

"Look at me, Mateo..."

My voice comes out soft and sweet—exactly how I hoped—but he doesn't look at me. For the first time since I met him, his thousand-yard stare is history, and he's gazing past me, nice and peaceful.

"That's right; just keep on looking at the ceiling if it cools your jets. And don't worry, you won't have to move your ass because I'm not going anywhere any time soon. If you fall asleep, well, that's no big deal at all." I stop babbling, and we both simply stare. I stare at him; he stares at...well, at nothing. Strange as fuck, but at least it's not awkward.

And damn, this man's got a one-in-a-billion kind of gorgeous thing going on. His eyes are a shade of brown too light to look human but surely are stunning. And stunning isn't normally in my vocabulary, but it's the only word that works for his cat eyes. Not to take anything away from the rest of his face, because it's perfect, too. Everything—straight nose, pointed chin, smooth skin, even the thick stubble on his cheeks. It all fits just right and is framed by silky golden-brown waves. I think he's about the prettiest person I've ever seen close up, except on a movie screen. Nope—changed my mind; he's prettier than the folks on movie screens too.

I've got no plans to look away from his eyes so I can gawk at his super-hot body. That wouldn't be classy. But I'm holding his strong shoulder right in my hands, and I've been rubbing his arm, off and on, for the last couple of minutes. I think if I wanted to, I could count all of the strands of muscle there.

How can it be that this beautiful man is so broken? Sure as shit, he's worse off than even me. The world doesn't want to let me be me, but this dude has suffered some serious shit, and it's left him halfway gone.

Chapter Three

MATT'S JOURNAL DATED JULY 2005

I'm supposed to write down my memories to get them off my chest and out of my head. I guess it can't hurt at this point, so here goes…

Daniel Blankenship took me when I was seven.

The asshole fucking dragged a little boy off his brand-new seventh-birthday BMX bike because he wanted a new toy. When he yanked me from my bike, and I saw it resting on the sidewalk, the front tire still spinning, my major concern was that if I left it there, some kid would come along and steal it. But when he stuffed me into his van, I quickly got the bigger picture. I was being stolen, and my bike was the least of my worries.

I do my best not to think about the things he did to me for the next eight years, until, at fifteen, I was too old to do it for him. So at this point, the twisted shit he did is tightly sealed in long-term storage—in a fireproof, waterproof unit at the very back of my brain—where I plan to leave it and forget I ever put it there. God knows I've recalled it all—every revolting detail—and I've suffered over each memory I fought my ass off to own. But I can't dwell on that shit anymore, or even talk about it, as everybody in my life seems so bound and determined to make me do.

I've reached the conclusion that I can no longer live in
the company of other people.

MATT

As is not unusual, I dreamt about the day I was torn off my
bike, ripped away from my mother and father and brothers,
my friends and teachers, my dog, and everything I knew and
loved.

Sliding off the couch, I spread my arms wide and bend
in half to rub my cramped calves. I'm weary from having
slept curled up in a ball on the couch, as I'm too tall a man
to get away with doing that. And this morning, I'm more
confused than usual. When I went to sleep, I wasn't alone,
which in itself is a complete departure from my usual
meticulously solitary routine.

Upon waking, I find no one else is here.

Vedie must have breathed a loud sigh of relief, having
escaped the loony bin unscathed. My solitary state should
come as a relief to me too, as it saves me from having to oust
Vedie from my apartment and somehow inform him he isn't
welcome to return. But strangely, all I feel this morning is
more hollow than usual.

I saunter to the kitchen, hoping a cup of orange juice
will provide me with the energy my stretching didn't, and
when I get there, I'm surprised to find the cats have been
fed. Vedie couldn't have left too long ago, as Jennifer and
Conan are seated in a patch of sunlight on the kitchen floor,
still performing their after-breakfast grooming. I want to be
angry he violated my privacy by rummaging through my
cabinets in search of cat food, but I can't muster up the
energy. I grab a mug, go to the fridge, pour the OJ, and when

I sit at the kitchen table to drink it, I see the note. It's written in pen on the back of a paper towel in the rounded flowery script of a high school girl, ostentatious in the austerity of my cottage.

> *Last night you were miles away. Not sure where you went to, but one second you were with me, and then you were gone. You probably don't remember it, but I stayed w/ you mostly until sunup. Hate to leave you right now, but I've got to work the breakfast shift. Come on over to the Tiki Hut if you're hungry, dude.*
>
> *V*

I owe Vedie an explanation for my disassociation last night, which is what my shrink used to call it when the connection between my mind and my body and the rest of the world got lost. Not that it's a huge deal for me—I've been zoning out for as long as I can remember.

VEDIE

"I didn't catch your last name, dude."

Can't believe he came here for breakfast. Never thought it'd happen, but Mateo is sitting right in front of me, eating scrambled eggs at the bar.

He cracks a smile. The dude should smile more, because seeing it's like chomping down on a mouthful of eye candy. "That's because I never told you."

"Ouch. You sure do know how to kick a guy."

I'm feeling all-boy right now. I'm wearing my tan shorts and my green work shirt, and I've got my high-tops on with white Nike crew socks sticking up. Not a hairband or a hint of lip gloss—tiny studs fill in all the holes in my ears instead of hoops and danglies. Dressed this way, I could pass for a tough guy, even back home.

"North...Matt North," he says real serious, like Bond... James Bond. And it's weird how he doesn't seem too freaked out that he let me hold him like he was a baby for most of last night. Probably, he doesn't remember it.

"North...as in, Up North, where I came from and am never going back to?" I ask and wink at him.

He smiles again, causing little Vedie to perk up in my pants. "Yeah," he says, his voice breathy. "Something like that."

"Hey, Vedie!! Spill on table twelve!" Angie hollers from halfway across the beach.

"I'm on it!" Mateo is watching me with his eerie, undead eyes. "Duty calls, man."

Before I have a chance to start the hike toward table twelve, which is practically on the water's edge, Mateo jumps off the bar stool and calls, "Wait up!"

Seeing as I wasn't on my way yet, I keep my feet planted on the sand.

"Come over to my place for a swim when you get off work."

"Love to, but I'm not too sure I remember the way." Wish I could say *Sure, I'll be there by three*, but it was dark when he drove me to his cottage last night, and I wasn't paying too much attention to the road. I barely managed to get back to town this morning.

"I'll wait for you and drive us there."

"You'll wait here? I'm not off until two."

Real slow—and I'm not lying when I say real shaky—he reaches over and touches my arm. "I don't mind waiting."

"I haven't got my swimsuit," I warn him.

I get one of those knock-me-flat smiles. "I'm not worried."

I can feel his golden eyes on me as I head over to clean up the big spill.

I DON'T MIND how we drive to his cottage in pin-drop silence. The wind is blowing in my hair, blustering so hard in the plain gray truck cab that it keeps on lifting my skirt up almost to my waist. But Mateo doesn't seem to notice my bare brown legs, shaved smooth, or my struggle to tame my flying skirt. He stares out the windshield like he's alone in the truck. Maybe he's in that same place he went last night when the lights behind his eyes went out.

When I arrived at the truck a little while ago wearing the flouncy, flowery mini skirt and a lacey halter-top, Mateo looked me up and down and nodded. I could practically see the words forming in his head: Vedie's feeling girly again.

But I didn't see anything in his expression in the way of judgment—no disgust or horniness, and probably most surprising to me, no look of "I wanna punch his lights out, because who does this dude think he is, trying to pass as a lady?" Even though I'm not actually trying to pass as a lady.

As soon as the truck stops, Mateo seems to remember he's not alone. He looks over at me and asks, "Want to go swimming?" His expression is blank; he probably couldn't care less about my answer.

"I'm not gonna go naked." Even though I say it soft, my words come out sounding kind of wiseass. I fold my arms across my chest.

"I'll find you something to wear."

I sit there shaking my head, busy worrying about what I'm gonna wear for swimming, until Mateo comes around to my side of the truck to get me out. When he helps me take the big step down out of the truck, my eyes burn. I get misty, just the way I did yesterday. It's just that Mateo's not like any other dude I've ever been with. Most think that because I'm a boy who's in touch with the girl inside him, I'm nothing but a bizarre sex toy, and not a real person. And it seems that guys who are into dudes like me, are in it mostly to get a freaky lay.

"No worries, Vedie." He offers me a half smile, and the sight of those white teeth makes me wonder about how they'd feel scraping on my tongue. I'm too classy to tell him so, but I've gotta bite my lip hard to keep it in.

I follow Mateo to his plain and simple cottage full of cats, and he heads right to his bedroom. He comes back with a thin white T-shirt and black boxer briefs.

"I think I can make this work," I tell him, even though I ain't so sure. I take the clothes from his hands.

"You know where the bathroom is...so..."

I head to the bathroom to change. After I strip off my skirt and pretty top and undies, I let them fall to the floor in a soft pile, but then pick them up and fold them nice and neat. I throw Mateo's V-neck T-shirt over my head. It's loose because I'm a skinny guy and don't have any big muscles like the ones that usually stretch this T-shirt. I tie the shirt off to the side, halfway up my belly, and let my shoulder poke out of the neck hole. I pull on the boxer briefs. They cling to my ass, which I've been told time and again is my best feature. Looking in the mirror over the sink, I see that my lips are still shiny and red, but my eyes are flat because I didn't heap on mascara, knowing I'd be swimming and it'd drip right down my face. Not a good look.

When I come out of the bathroom, I'm faced with a totally hot man dressed in a pair of faded navy-blue swim trunks, tied low on slim hips, and a loose tank top. He's the type of man that, until now, I only dreamed about being with. All I can think is, "You must pump iron, dude." And so I say it. I kind of operate that way.

He laughs, and it sounds deep and sexy, and when it stops, I wanna hear it all over again. "My weight bench is on the screened porch. I guess I do spend a lot of time out there." He looks at the floor instead of at me. "You comfortable in that T-shirt?"

"Yeah. It'll work fine."

Without another word, Mateo pats the heads of each member of our kitty audience and makes for the door. "Come on." He opens the door for me and lets me pass by. I get these tingling feelings all over my chest because he treats me so polite.

On his private beach, I find myself wondering how he can afford to pay for this pricey waterfront joint. But I don't ask him because I'm no gold digger. I dip my toe in, and the water is the same temperature as the warm air, but it still feels cool on my skin. I step in real easy. Mateo trots right past me and dives.

I walk out to where it's waist-deep and then sink super slow down to my neck. He swims a bunch of laps while I lie here and float. His laps are frenzied—a sort of nervous pacing—but in the water instead of on the sand. Finally, I swim out to him and he slows, then stops.

"Why'd you invite me here?" I demand, sounding sort of bitchy.

He looks surprised for a second but only shrugs. Then he says real quiet, "Because you don't scare me."

Well, I won't say it's the best compliment I've ever got, but I'll take it.

Not to say I don't stop and wonder why a guy Mateo's size would be scared of anybody who doesn't have a gun.

"But what do you want with me?" That came out wrong. I sigh. "What I mean is, when I first hit on you, I looked all-boy. So what're you doing here with me, now that I'm looking like a girl?"

As he treads water, Mateo's golden gaze meets with mine, and there's a click in the air between us. "I'm not all that worried about how you express your gender."

Huh? "Come on, man, face it—you were standing outside The Only Tiki Hut waiting on the guy who came on to you in the restaurant. And somebody dressed all girly came out instead."

"Makes no difference to me."

"Well, if you showed up at the bar today in a party dress and a strand of pearls, it would've made a big difference to me!" I'm a dude who's into dudes who look like dudes, and it's that simple.

"That's you... Don't analyze me too much, Vedie, and I'll grant you the same favor." His eyes look scared, and they shut real slow. When they open up, he looks brave again. "I like the way you are."

Well, that's good enough for me, so I move on to my next question. "Can I touch you?" It's forward to ask this, but I don't much care.

Mateo's head slips down beneath the surface of the water. When he comes up, he shakes the hair off his face, takes a deep breath and swallows hard, and finally nods so small I can hardly see. "Let's go up onto the beach."

We swim to shore with the waves, and in these skimpy briefs I know there's no way I can hide that I'm seriously turned on. And maybe I'm feeling on the feminine side right now, but I'm not a girl, so I've got nothing against my dick.

I thought this subject through, long and hard, because guys like me who risk everything to dress pretty in public can't pretend it's not a real part of me. And this part of me is most of the reason why I'm not living in a closet up in Boston right now. Up North or down South, I'm gay as the day is long—but I can be as much like a girl as I wanna be down here, even if I've got a boy's equipment.

Mateo lingers behind me until I get out of the water, and then he follows me up the beach where he grabs a couple of huge brown towels out of a basket and hands me one. We dry off and spread them out to lie on the sand. Me and him stretch out flat on our backs, and, at first, it's pretty awkward. I'm reminded of how it felt to be a teenage boy on my first secret hookup with another teenage boy, who'd deny he got with me until the day he died. But I can't hold back, and I slide his way and press the whole front of me against them soft light-brown curls that whisper all over his chest. And shit—the guy jolts to the side about a mile when my wet T-shirt touches his tanned skin. Lucky for me, after a couple of seconds, he moves back over.

"Kiss me, Teo," I say in my sweetest voice.

For a minute, the light behind his eyes dims, and I think he's going to leave me the way he did last night. But after the light flickers, it comes back, and his eyes look bright again. Real slow, he leans over me and lowers his head until our lips meet. Then he kisses me a half dozen times, all of them deep. Not sure why, but my lips are shaking. I don't fall behind, though—even shaky, I can keep up. But when I try to put my hands on his back, he squirms in a bad way, so I just drop my arms to my sides.

"How, uh... Vedie, how do you...like to be touched?" Mateo's probably not too sure if I think of myself as a girl or a guy. And my mouth falls open; I'm pretty shocked he even asked me this, seeing as most guys just go for what they want.

So I reach up and turn his head to the side, brush the long damp hair off his ear, and whisper my best explanation for how I am. "I'm a dude, Mateo. I get into feeling pretty sometimes...and there's a big part of me that's gentle and sensitive...and I like how that part of me sees the world. But I'm still a man." I gulp loud because this much honesty could get me killed.

No sooner do I utter this truth, though, then his hands rise to my chest. His tongue is back in my mouth by the time he starts to feel me up.

There's not much for him to play with on my chest, but he seems cool with what I've got. Soon he's pushing my T-shirt up around my neck, and his mouth slides down my neck until he's latched onto my left side. I never felt as if a man actually understood me before right now, with Mateo's needy mouth on my nipple, sucking me hard between his teeth. Mateo gets how there's plenty of lady's feelings mixed into my kind of manliness.

Finally, he asks, "Can I use my hand on you...down there?"

I know what he's asking me—if I like to be touched the same way other guys do. I can hardly believe he's pushing his own needs to the side long enough to check. Heat rushes to my face as I drag his big hand down my body toward my junk. "I'm into what you're into."

He nods against my chest and then pushes the black briefs down my thighs and flings them into the sand. "You're so beautiful, Vedie...so sexy." His fingers are on my dick, rubbing circles on top where it's smooth, and then reaching lower to stroke more of my length. At the same time, his dick is poking hard into the side of my butt.

"Teo..." I slide into the secret space in my head I usually save for when I'm all alone in my bed, fantasizing about making it with a man like him. But when I try to reach around his back and hold him, he again wiggles away.

"I want to make you come." He doesn't say *jerk you off*. Even now, when he's so turned on, eyes squinting and teeth gritted, he doesn't treat me like he thinks I'm a slut.

I throw back my head when he reaches down to my balls and pulls up, his fingers wrapped tight around me. "Oh, my God. oh...sh-shit." Mateo strokes me just the way I like it. I can't help but groan because it's the best feeling I've had in what seems like forever.

"That's right, Vedie, give it all to me," he murmurs, and it only takes a minute or two for me to give him exactly what he asked for.

After I come into his hand, Mateo leans over me—his gaze glued to mine—and I wonder what comes next. I'm still panting from how good he made me feel, but I need to find out what I can do for him. "Can I kiss...can I kiss you down here?" I drop my hand onto the tent that's popped up in the front of his swim trunks. "I want to so bad."

Mateo doesn't answer in words. First he shudders. In his eyes, there's a faraway look, and I suspect he's not one hundred percent here with me on the breezy beach. I'd bet my ass that the biggest part of Mateo is now hovering about ten feet in the air, looking down on us as we get busy on the beach. I'm surprised when he whispers, "Yes. I want it. I... Vedie, I want you."

And boom, he falls flat on his back and pulls off his trunks. I climb between his legs and look at my prize—so big and thick and impatient. And I dive down and go to town. I get into the feeling of his stiff dick sliding down my throat, and the needy sounds that come outta him with every flick of my tongue almost make me come again. But what's best is how he shows me he likes my mouth, by brushing the sides of my face with his fingertips. As if I'm the only one who can make him feel this good.

He squirts in my mouth—I even frown when he's doing it, not because I don't like his taste, but because it's over way too quick. And then a trigger in my brain snaps me back to the here and now. Some dudes get pissed off when the deed is done, and I've gotta be ready. I admit I've got no clue what's going to come next with Mateo and me. Maybe he'll never come back to The Only Tiki Hut, and I'll never see him again, but I don't get the feeling he has a mind to beat my ass because I'm not a girl.

The sun is warm on my skin, and I think I'd be able to relax if I could strike that panicked look from Mateo's pretty eyes. So I drop down onto the sand on my belly, toss one arm over his chest, stick the other under his neck, and holding him tight, I drift away

Chapter Four

MATT'S JOURNAL DATED JULY 2006

"I'm back."

I've been thinking a lot about the day I went home at the age of fifteen. Daniel dropped me off on the corner of my street and said, "I should kill you, but I'm gonna let you go home. So get out." I didn't say a word, no "thank you for letting me live" or "you're a pervert and I hate you." I got my ass out of his van, walked slowly along the sidewalk—I even dragged my feet, I think—until I reached a big yellow house I vaguely recognized. Before knocking on the door, I looked back to where Daniel's van had been parked on the street. It was gone, so I had no choice but to rap my knuckles against the wood, and when my mother answered, I simply said, "I'm back." I tuned out her screams and numbed my body to her embrace.

And a long, horrible nightmare was over.

The thing is, the Matthew North who'd been abducted eight years before was not the boy who returned to his family. The Matthew who walked back into that big yellow house was nothing but a human scab. What looked like a normal teenage boy—granted I was pierced and tattooed and wore a mullet—was nothing but living, breathing scar tissue. A few months of therapy to help me "reintegrate to a normal lifestyle" led to a year during which the main objective was to keep me from hanging myself in my bedroom closet. The memories I'd blocked came trickling and then pouring back into my scar tissue brain. The suicide-prevention-year, as I've come to call it, was followed by a period of time when I lived away at a "special" school, during which I ingested huge quantities of antidepressants and received extensive counseling for PTSD. And much of this fun stuff occurred in the glare of the media spotlight. It seemed Matthew North, abducted child who miraculously returned home after eight years, was everybody's business.

The only thing that has given me any peace was leaving home. Getting away from people who care for the wrong reasons and show it in the wrong ways, from my public "stolen boy" persona, from journalists whose only goal was to get the rights to the miniseries.

I've been on Placida Island for a year now, and I think I'm almost a person again. I've arranged my life so I'm rarely required to experience emotions or deal with people and situations I find uncomfortable.

Things are bad, but better now.

ALMOST TEN YEARS ago, I separated from my family and a world I could no longer relate to.

I kept myself isolated...until now.

And here I am.

I have not been held in a caring human being's arms for over twenty years. For some of the two interim decades, the arms that held me belonged to a human being who didn't care but simply used me for sexual gratification. And during the rest of those long years, I refused to allow the arms of those who said they really did care to get anywhere near me.

And here I am. Held in arms that won't let go.

After a few minutes of this tender human contact, I manage to extricate myself from Vedie's arms without waking him. I now stand, my tank top hanging loosely on my damp chest and covering most of what needs to be hidden, with my feet in the surf, staring down upon the naked man on my beach. He's fast asleep on his belly, his round, brown backside dusted with sand, mooning the sun without apology. Asleep, he looks beautiful and innocent, and at a quick glance, I see a guileless teenage boy. He must be nineteen or so...possibly twenty, but not much older.

I felt as if I was a real person with Vedie. I forgot to be Crazy Matt for a lazy afternoon, but now I'm wondering what the hell I'm doing here with him...or with her...not that gender makes much of a difference to my quandary. *Don't trust anybody* has been my motto since a July day when I was seven years old and my world turned upside down and inside out.

Am I actually trying to forge some sort of a relationship with a person who, like me, isn't real—and can't ever be real because the reality of who we are is broken and ruined and wrong, and doesn't fit into society?

I dig my toes into the wet sand as a large wave washes back into the sea, pulling away all the sand except what's beneath my feet. Standing on a tiny island, I allow myself to wonder. What is Vedie trying to accomplish here—making love to a broken man with a femininity many would question, on a remote beach off a rarely traveled dirt road, on an island where all the misfit toys like us have come to live?

I stifle a snort of laughter when I realize that he trusts me. This Vedie...this sensitive young man who is sound asleep, naked except for the white T-shirt twisted loosely around his neck, who voluntarily came to this desolate place with me, a virtual stranger, trusting that I wouldn't harm him... That I wouldn't beat him and rape him and torture him as Daniel did to me for so many years. And he trusted me with his greatest secrets—how he likes to be touched and how he wants to see the world. I shake my head, because he's a fool. But so am I, because when I made love to him with my hands, he returned the favor with his mouth. He was exactly as gentle and sweet and feminine as he had hoped, not only in his mind, but in mine as well.

I step off the tiny sand island in the waves and drop down beside my slumbering guest, now certain it's time for him to leave my hideaway...my solitary escape. He's in danger here—in danger of falling for a man with no soul.

But even if I want to assert that it's Vedie I'll be protecting when I drive him away, dump him on a sidewalk, and warn him never to return, I'm more truly protecting myself from the pain of a potential attachment. Because I learned very young that no relationship is permanent. Those I endeavor to love will be ripped away from me cruelly; it's far better to be alone and comfortably numb than to be alone and wrapped in total devastation.

This time, when I stand, my heart doesn't rise with the rest of my body; it remains on the ground, buried in a pile of damp sand.

VEDIE

I'm feeling all-dude on the ride home.

To be real, when I woke up from my nap on the beach and saw *what the fuck* in Mateo's eyes, I made a mad, naked dash for the bathroom, grabbed the tan shorts from work out of my pack, and stuck them on. Shit rolls off me easier when I'm feeling macho, and I know deep down, I'm not gonna care too much for whatever Mateo's gonna tell me in his truck. So this is how it has to be.

"Hope you don't mind I'm borrowing your T-shirt." There's no way on earth I'm going to put my lacy top back on, seeing as when I'm wearing girls' clothes I'm more sensitive to shit that gets hurled my way. I untie the shirt and let it hang halfway down my thighs.

"It's fine. You can keep it."

Shit. This dude's done with me for real. It's fuckin' amazing what a good come'll do for a guy. After the big moment, an easy sucker like me doesn't even exist anymore. Hadn't figured Mateo was one of those guys. Shows what a dumbass I am.

"Sure. I gotcha."

Sitting in the truck, I cross my legs tight, fold my arms over my chest, and turn to stare out the window, all pissed off and bitchy. But since I badly don't want to cry, I change my game plan. I spread my legs wide and slump over, playing the role of the angry freak I had no choice but to play in high school.

"Can you bring me back to The Only Tiki Hut? I left my bike there."

"Let me pick up your bike and give you a lift home. It's not a problem."

"So chivalry's not dead after all," I mumble.

"It's not like that, Vedie." Mateo glances across the cab of the truck at me.

I think I see pain in his eyes, and I don't get it. "It's not like what?"

"We—the two of us—aren't going to work out together."

"It's not me, it's you, right, man?" I make an attempt to smile, but it doesn't fly. Still, I push the soft part of Vedie back even further because there's no way I'm going to cry in this motherfuckin' truck.

"And you can't come back to my place again."

"No shit, Sherlock. I've got zero sense of direction... couldn't find my way back to your house if you paid me."

"It's just I...uh..."

"Save it, Mateo." I turn toward the window and close my eyes, wishing to hell I had a ball cap to pull down over my face. "Wake me up when we get there."

I'VE GOT A tiny room over the Placida Island Laundry-Zone. It's not much, but it's mine, and I'm cool with it. I share a bathroom with two other dudes who live in the single units on each side of mine. It's not so bad, and it's way better than checking behind my back all the time like I had to do in Boston.

When I'm here, I'm usually alone and I've got nothing to prove, so I made my surroundings as pretty and peaceful as I wanted. I got some petal-pink paint on sale at the hardware store and knocked myself out painting the walls. I found these shiny silver star stickers in a BOGO bin at a gift shop, and I stuck them all over the place when the paint was dry. The walls look pink and shimmery, exactly like the inside of my head when my mood is soft and silky and sweet. Don't have a bedspread yet—too short on cash. So I superglued some rainbow patches I took with me from

Boston to cover the stains on a used set of light-pink sheets I picked up at a thrift shop for one buck. Works for me. Next thing on my home-beautiful list is a couple yards of lime-green tulle for curtains.

I stare into the mirror over the sink while I towel dry my wild-ass hair. It looks like a fuckin' huge bush tonight because my dreads are coming loose. Gotta clean them up sometime soon. But for now, I pat them down.

Aqua-green eyes on a black man aren't exactly rare, but you don't see them every day. Back in school, I used to hate my eyes, seeing as they gave away my secret—that most of my insides are soft and light, not sharp and bold. With one look at these eyes, my brothers and cousins knew I wasn't badass enough, and they set about trying to toughen me up. It didn't work, though. I don't think you can scare the softness out of somebody when softness is most of who he is.

But since last weekend when I got busy with Mateo on the beach—the day I let him use me and totally got into it—I've been feeling sort of slutty. In fact, I've never felt this worthless in my life. Guess I thought shit was gonna be different with Mateo—he seemed so kind. I've been wrong before, but this time, being wrong stings.

Don't think I'm gonna fuck around with any more dudes for a while.

It's time for work. Hope to hell Joey keeps his paws off me tonight. His groping is getting old fast.

MATT

There's something about Vedie, I think as I drive my truck over the bridge, leading me off the island.

I'm not saying I regret doing what I did—telling the kid to keep his distance—but if I were an honest man, I'd say I feel a certain emptiness when I drive past The Only Tiki Hut and spot his old BMX chained to the bike rack. I think of eyes that can't help but smile, and the risk he took in telling me how he wanted it to go when we fooled around on the beach, and how he held me and asked no questions when I mentally vacated the premises. But since I'm a man in hiding, I say to myself, *there's something about Vedie*, and I leave it there.

Strange, but I'm missing The Only Tiki Hut, too. For almost a decade I've kept to myself, worked my online marketing job, played with my cats, pumped iron on my porch, and grabbed a few decent meals each week at the tiki bar on the bay. I don't interact with many people, which is by design. I get my fill of being in the presence of human beings by visiting the one and only restaurant on Placida Island. But, for all intents and purposes, you could say I fucked the busboy and then dumped him on his ass, so I've earned myself a long drive off the island every time I'm in the mood for meatloaf.

VEDIE

"What're you doing here?" I open the door to my apartment and there's Joey, standing on my doorstep with his legs wide apart, hands on his hips, bending a little bit to the right as he peers inside.

"Well, dat's not a very nice way to greet a man who came here to visit ya, little girl." Seems as if Joey doesn't know where to look first, seeing as I'm wearing short cutoff jeans and a tight yellow belly shirt. "Can I come in, sweetheart?"

"Um...look Joey, I'm busy decorating." I get the same bad feeling as when my cousin's best friend Juan came around my house back in Boston, before I got booted. When my cousin, James, and my brothers were around, Juan acted like he wanted to kick my ass—same as all of the rest of them—but when we were alone, he checked me out the same way Joey's checking me out right now. And he drooled the same way too.

"Lemme help." He looks inside and sees the ladder I borrowed from my neighbor leaning against the wall. "You hanging a mirror on the ceiling over your bed? I'll just bet you are...and that's my kinda kinky!"

I step back and push hard on the door. "You oughta go home to your wife—hang a mirror over your marriage bed, huh?"

But he sticks his damn foot in the door before I can slam it shut. "I don't think I like your attitude!" he yells in my face, and I smell stale booze breath.

Lucky for me, my neighbor Pete comes up the stairs and hears Joey hollering. "What's going on out here? You okay, Vedie?"

"Um, I'm okay. And my friend here was just leaving. Ain't that right, Joey?"

Joey's pissed off to no end, but he pulls back his stupid foot. "See ya at work, cocktease."

He glares into my eyes one more time and shakes his head like *I* was the one who did something bad to him. Then he stomps down the stairs.

Maybe this island isn't gonna work any better for me than Boston did.

MATT

Alone feels different today.

Before I invited Vedie back to my beachfront cottage, let him see the simple surroundings where I pass my days and get a taste of how I live, I was alone entirely by choice. I methodically set up every part of my life—work, play, how and where I ate meals—with the intention of doing it all by myself. In fact, the only times I left the solitary comfort of my own home was when I was in need of supplies, or to get a better meal than I could make in my own kitchen. And I ventured to The Only Tiki Hut when I was in the mood for a brief and nonthreatening reminder that I wasn't completely alone on the planet. But today, solitary comfort feels strangely like solitary confinement.

"It was my choice." I say this to Conan and Jennifer who are stalking a gecko on the rocks that separate the grass from the beach. As if a couple of cats care why Vedie isn't frolicking along with them on the beach, and their owner is, as usual, standing in the surf alone.

"Why does it feel as if he rejected me?" Conan looks up at me, tilts his head, and meows. And then his attention returns to the gecko Jennifer now thinks she has cornered.

She'll soon learn what I've come to know—things don't always unfold as you expect them to.

I turn around and slowly wade out into the water until I'm waist-deep and contemplating a dive. I wish when the salt water washes over me, it could wash away my frenzied thoughts—my guilt, my disappointment, and the rage I've condemned myself to endure in this isolated life. But I already know it won't change anything because I'm not capable of doing what's necessary to bond in a meaningful way with another human being.

I dive into the water and kick hard so I sink enough to push my fingers through the sand. This refreshing plunge will hopefully be enough to stop the cycle of my obsessive thinking.

But by the time my face breaks the surface of the water my lips are moving and my thoughts are rambling with the sort of messy notions that make me want to escape from my very own island retreat. I'm owned by the insistent thoughts of a textbook-case depressed, phobic, obsessive-compulsive adult survivor of physical and sexual abuse and neglect. I can't quiet my mind; I can't still my lips. And I stopped trying to fix this broken part of me years ago.

Doing laps—speedy and frantic strokes that easily part the dense salt water in my path—goes a long way toward reaching my goal, which is to exhaust my body enough so I'm literally too weary to become trapped in yet another maze of thought. But before fatigue sets in, there's plenty of time to accept that the avoidance tactics I used in childhood to help me cope with the abuse are not particularly conducive to healthy adult interactions.

This is an understatement of immense proportions.

I swim a length of the beach in what feels like record time. And I think.

I am an avoider of all things emotional.

I depend on no one but myself.

I am as secretive as I am cold.

No family, no friends, and, God forbid, no lovers.

I take my next lap more slowly. There's no rush today.

For the first time in ten years, I stuck my toe in to test the waters of friendship. But instead of stepping into the ocean because it was as warm and welcoming as I'd hoped, I flopped down onto my belly and let the waves wash my chance of bonding with Vedie out to sea.

None of these rambling admissions stops me from mourning the spark of elation I'd experienced at connecting, even briefly, with Vedie. None of my efforts to convince myself I want to spend my life alone is enough to squelch the glimmer of hope that I'll have a chance to spend another day with the only person who ever managed to sidestep my sidestepping.

I swim two more lengths of the beach, using every bit of energy and power I possess.

Maybe I made a mistake. Maybe I screwed up by casting him away. Maybe I want him back.

Maybe I'll stay here alone in comfortable solitary confinement where I'm safe.

MATT'S JOURNAL DATED FEBRUARY 2007

I learned a lot in my seventh year of life. A very harsh year it was.

First, I learned I was completely powerless. Daniel could do whatever he wanted to me and there wasn't one goddamned thing I could do to stop it. No amount of kicking, screaming, scratching, crying, or begging made a dent in Daniel's resolve to satisfy his warped desires on my seven-year-old body.

Once I admitted this, my next lesson was relatively easy: embrace the helplessness.

Hold on to the helplessness, Matthew, I told myself. Grip it tight and make it your own, because no matter what you do, your pain won't cease.

Figure out how to make helplessness work for you.

By the time I turned eight, I just didn't care. Ever seen an eight-year-old boy who couldn't give a crap about video games or pizza parties or baseball? I'll be the first to say it's a sad sight. Don't have hope—this became the law of my life. Be invisible—another hard, fast rule. And when the world notices you, Mark (the name Daniel gave to me), show them that nothing they think, say, or do affects you. Lots of shrugging and eye-rolling was involved in this part, if I remember correctly. I told myself—eat whenever there's food around, sleep whenever you can find a flat surface, as long as Daniel's passed out cold. Watch as much TV as is humanly possible because there's no better or more painless way to make time fly.

But as I live my life on Placida Island, I try not to embrace helplessness anymore. Only problem is the lessons I learned during my seventh year of life have proven to be impossible to forget.

Chapter Five

MATT

It's been almost two weeks since I've been to The Only Tiki Hut on Placida Island. I'm hoping my absence has allowed Vedie sufficient time to forget about my existence, because it is what's fair. Ironically, absence has made my heart only grow fonder of the very few memories I have of him. They're quite vivid in my mind, probably because I have no other recollection of recent human interaction to offset their impact. Nonetheless, I'm now heading over to The Only Tiki Hut to eat some dinner in the presence of the restaurant and bar staff, who know me very vaguely, but are the closest thing I have to a family.

I park my truck in my usual corner spot of the parking lot. Walking past the bike rack, I'm simultaneously relieved and disappointed there is no lime-green-and-white BMX bike in sight.

"I'm not here to see him," I remind myself and make my way to an empty table for two near the restrooms. I turn my chair toward the ocean. This usually works to calm me.

"Heya, Matt!" Sheila speaks when she's still several feet away, and although I nearly leap out of my skin from the shock of it, I realize she's making an effort to warn me of her approach so I don't startle like a newborn. Last time she came to my table completely unannounced, I lurched forward and spilled my water everywhere. "You haven't been around in ages."

"Been busy."

She smiles. "You drinking water tonight?"

I don't even need to speak; Sheila has "catering to Crazy Matt" mastered as if she were put on earth just to serve me. All that's required of me is to nod, and so I do. I should really thank the woman for years of intuitive service, but I'm still reeling from having been surprised by her very unsurprising entrance. I'll add a few bucks to her tip, instead.

But something's wrong here. Usually a busboy greets me and brings my first drink to the table. Tonight Sheila is, apparently, acting as both busboy and waiter. I look around uneasily, unaccustomed to even slight changes in my routine. For almost ten years, the drill hasn't changed, and a busboy always greets me and delivers the first drink.

I must appear perplexed because Sheila's tone is comforting. "I know, having no busboy is strange for me, too, hun. But somebody poked holes in both tires on Vedie's bike, and he had to walk to work, so he's gonna be late."

I nod again, as I wonder who would do such a thing to his bike. My fists have curved into angry balls on the tabletop. Perspiration gathers on my forehead. Doing my best to ignore this visceral reaction to Vedie's plight, I concentrate on sipping my water while I watch a woman gently scoop her young son from the distant waves.

I must push what happened to Vedie's bike out of my mind. It is, after all, none of my business.

"Sorry for being late, Angie. I'll get my bike fixed tomorrow after work. Think I'm gonna need new tires altogether."

It's his voice, already sounding drained and weary, which sucks because he's just starting his shift. Not that I give a shit.

"Well, you've never been late before, so I'm not going to count this time against you. Go ahead and take tomorrow morning off to get your bike fixed. I'll put you on for another shift later this week. How's that?" Angie's reasonable and I'm unreasonably glad.

"Works for me. I better get my ass in gear." He is presenting himself as the same young man I first met at the bar. I want to turn around and stare at him because I appreciate the way he looks when he's manly as much as when he's ladylike, not that I plan to ask myself why. I turn my chair to face the bar as I wait for my drink, allowing my eyes to follow him and the other busboy, Vinny, as they dart around, clearing tables and delivering drinks.

It takes at least ten minutes for Vedie to notice me, and when he does, he nearly trips over his feet. After recovering, he waves casually and shouts in my direction, "Hey, Mateo. Long time, no see." Then he heads to the bar to pick up some drinks.

It's business as usual for Vedie.

Sheila takes my dinner order, but my heart pounds fiercely. Again, I experience both intense relief and unreasonable disappointment at Vedie's lack of reaction to my presence. My connection with the world becomes hazy, and the racing thoughts that usually lead me to complete emotional withdrawal shuffle into my brain as if they have a plan to take me away. This rarely happens in public.

What the fuck am I doing here? Why am I tempting myself by staring at him and pining over what can never be? I can't do the relationship thing, even if I want to.

The world dims even further as obsessive thoughts push everything else aside, and soon I experience the familiar sense that both my mind and body are growing numb. I begin to separate from the goings-on at the tropical tiki hut.

"I'm not a girl!"

This shout draws me back.

"Listen to me—I said I'm not a girl!" Vedie's agitated voice coming from the direction of the men's bathroom grabs my attention. "And even if I was, I wouldn't wanna get groped by *you*!"

"Just because you aren't in one of your hooker getups don't mean you ain't dat same whore who leaves here every night wanting to get fucked by the first guy you bump into!"

"Come on, Joey...you're getting out of hand here..." His tone has shifted into pleading.

Not only have I returned to the here and now, but I'm paying close attention—even straining to hear more of the fucked-up conversation coming from the men's room.

"Get your damn paws off me! Let me go!" And he's frantic again.

"Ahhh...finally, got my hands on the finest ass on the island. Hey, don't be like dat, sweetheart! You know you want it..."

"Stop it, man...no... *I said no!*"

No...no...no. The word rings in my head.

No. I'd said it to Daniel a thousand times. He'd never once listened. And I'm not going to sit here and listen as some guy assaults Vedie.

I leap to my feet and run into the bathroom, stopping short at the sight before me. Joey's got Vedie bent over the sink, his shorts drooping around his ankles. The older man is simultaneously pressing on the back of his neck with one hand to hold him down and squeezing his ass with the other. And he's grinning.

"For fuck's sake, let the kid go!" My bark is ferocious, which surprises me.

Joey keeps on squeezing. "You had your turn playing with the whore—now it's mine!"

I can't see Vedie's eyes, and I'm glad, because I know the shattered fear there would definitely push me over the edge. Instead of reaching out to drag him from under the asshole, I draw back my fist and punch the asshole's left cheek with everything in me. It feels so damn good I reach back and do it again a couple inches lower. With the second blow, Joey releases Vedie to clutch his jaw, which is when I grab the kid by the wrist and pull him against me.

I recognize the hollow look in Vedie's eyes; I've seen it in my own in the mirror too many times to count. "My shorts, Teo...my shorts..." he utters without expression. I lean down, grab his shorts and briefs, and drag them up around his waist, but he says it again. "My shorts..."

Vedie's probably in shock, so I tell him, "Your shorts are fine now. Come on, let's get out of here."

Vedie doesn't make a move toward the bathroom door, though. He stands beside me with wide, empty eyes, staring at Joey, who's now studying the floor. But the asshole gathers his senses quickly enough.

"Vedie knows I was only kidding around with him...right, darlin'?"

Although Vedie has no reaction, Joey's words infuriate me. "You were sexually assaulting him! Vedie, it's time to call the police!" I'm wild with fury, trapped somewhere between remembering my own horror and sympathizing with Vedie's. I rub briskly at my neck to ease the wary prickling of my skin, but it does nothing in the way of calming me.

My suggestion seems to break into Vedie's awareness. "No...no cops, Mateo. Will you just drive me home?" He's shook up, and I don't blame him. "I'm gonna go ask Angie if I can leave." He floats out of the bathroom the same way I float out of my body when a situation is too stressful.

"Don't go thinking this is over," I warn Joey, who's now leaning against the edge of the sink. "I saw what was happening in here."

The man straightens up and cracks a conspiratorial smile. "What're you so bent out of shape about? I'm just the same as you, man—I wanna take a walk on the wild side with a girly-boy who'll surely have the sucking power of a Hoover vacuum cleaner." He turns around, bends down to the sink, and throws water on his face. "And with an ass like dat, I don't give a shit what's dangling between his legs up front, know what I'm saying?"

His words burn through what little is left of my patience. If I stay in this bathroom with the asshole for one more second, I'll kill him. Since it's in nobody's best interest that I commit murder tonight, I turn around quickly and leave the bathroom. Vedie is talking to Angie at the bar.

"You were late for work today, and now you're not feeling good, so you want to leave early? Jeez, Vedie! This doesn't look good for you."

"Give me tonight and tomorrow to get my act together, and I swear I'll never make you wish you didn't hire me again!"

I thought I was already about as angry as I'd allow myself to get, especially on behalf of another person, until I stand here and watch him beg for his job. Seeing him pleading for one more chance riles me up, and the rule I set as a child, to block all intense emotions, is history. I head over to help him explain what happened in the men's room, but he catches my eye and very slowly shakes his head. So I stop, because I remember how it feels to be a victim and to take the blame. And to feel the shame.

Sheila approaches with my dinner all boxed and bagged to take with me. "Look, Matt, I know what's up with that pervert, Joey, and poor Vedie. Joey's on his ass all the time, because he's bi-curious or threatened or... Well, I know he's the one who popped Vedie's tires—and I'm gonna tell Angie this, too. Just promise me you'll get him home safe tonight." She hands me the bag and smiles as if I'm a friend. "I put some of his favorites in here, too. Take care of him, okay?"

I nod without catching her eye and lean on the far end of the bar waiting for him to be excused from work.

VEDIE

We don't say a word to each other until we're in the truck. "I-I wasn't ready...you know, I wasn't ready for Joey to come on to me." When I finally look at Mateo, I notice his eyes seem darker than usual. They scare me a little, so I look away.

"Why weren't you ready?"

"You saw me. I was at work—and I stopped in the men's room just to take a quick piss. I was wearing my shorts and work T-shirt. And I wasn't flirting or dressed sexy and asking to be messed with."

"He shouldn't be harassing you whether you're in shorts or a skirt, Vedie. Nothing you wear could possibly suggest that you're asking for it. And he wasn't merely harassing you, he was assaulting you."

I'm surprised: Mateo's voice is shaking almost as much as mine. I try to shrug it off, seeing as I never got too much respect from anybody, not even from Mateo. He dumped me the same afternoon I gave him my best blow job.

"It's cool of you to bring me home." I glance at him again and try to put a sincere "thank you for saving my ass, dude" in my expression.

He looks back at me, tilts his head, slows the car down, and pulls off the side of the road. "I, uh, I thought you might want to come over to my place tonight. You had a rough night and…and Sheila packed us dinner…and I thought we could hang out. It'll keep your mind off what happened, and we can talk about making that call to the police."

"I don't need you to do me any more favors, man. I'll be fine." I pat down my hair and add, "I live downtown, above the laundry place, remember?"

He shrugs and pulls back onto the road. Silence again, but I'm fine with it. Just because he gave a shit and stopped me from getting raped doesn't mean he cares for me the way I want to be cared for.

We pull up in front of my place, and who's parked outside on the street? Pervy Joey, or so Sheila calls him. "Shit," pops out of my mouth. I can't think of anything else to say.

When Joey sees me, he jumps out of his car and bolts to Mateo's truck, waving his arms like he's mad as a hornet. "Get out, bitch! I got shit to say to you!"

I roll up the window and yell through the glass, "Well, I've got nothing to say to you! Take a freaking hike!"

"You nearly got me fired—that piece-of-work Sheila told Angie I was always sniffing 'round you like a dog. Because of that—*because of you*—I got asked to leave for the night, and I got a warning *in writing*! If I screw up at all, I'm out the door on my ass!" His face is twisted, reminding me of my brother Tyrone's the time I told him I like to wear ladies' yoga pants when I'm kicking back in front of the television.

And I'm about to shit a brick I'm so scared, but this sort of scene isn't anything new to me. I've been here before. Pretty sure I'll be here again, too—because I'm a special breed of different. I'm trying to walk a fine line between showing myself as a dude and a lady, and it pisses folks off. So I dig down deep for courage. *What choice have I got?* Time's come for me to get my ass out of this truck and face the music.

"Thanks for the lift, Mateo." But before I have a chance to get out, he tears onto the road with a loud screech. Probably left a stripe of burned rubber on the tar.

"You're staying at my place tonight."

And just like that, he's driving and we get back to silence. I roll down the window and let the wind blow in my ears and block out the world.

MATT

"I'm not gonna fuck around with you tonight, Mateo, because, see—I'm no slut." Vedie's glaring at me with his arms crossed in front of him. He hasn't made the shift to seeming more feminine, and I've never spent time with him outside of work when he's this way.

"I didn't ask you to." I take the boxed food from the restaurant out of the bag and place it on the counter. "Sheila told me she packed some of your favorites."

He perks up. "Grilled cheese and fries—and cucumbers!"

Something so simple as a fucking grilled cheese sandwich and a pile of cucumbers makes Vedie excited enough to push a sexual assault to the back of his mind. I appreciate that he's uncomplicated, but still, I worry for him. I worry too much about safety, and he doesn't worry enough.

I open up my box, pull out a fish taco, and take a bite. Wonders never cease: I'm alone with another man, and I'm still fully present here in my kitchen. Under the table, Jennifer and Conan aggressively rub against our legs, and we suck down our food out of plastic containers like two starving teenage boys.

Right after we finish eating, Vedie grabs his backpack and asks, "Can I use the bathroom?"

I nod and start cleaning up the table as he heads down the short hall. Five minutes later, he returns, hair pulled back in a stretchy pink band and wearing just the T-shirt he'd borrowed from me.

"Hey, Mateo." He's different now, but the change is subtle. Vedie's head is tilted gracefully—when he walks it's almost as if he's floating—and his voice is a little bit softer. "I washed this T-shirt, and I've been carrying it with me for two weeks now so I could give it back to you. And here I am wearing it again."

"I told you before to consider it yours." And Vedie's more relaxed now, which relaxes me. "Want a beer? But I should ask this time, are you even old enough to drink alcohol?"

"I'm twenty-one. I look young, everybody says, but I'm plenty old to drink a beer, and after tonight, I definitely could go for a couple."

I grab two beers from the refrigerator. "Then let's sit down in the living room and drink these. Do you want a glass?" Vedie shakes his head and follows me to the living room, walking silently on bare feet. He sits on the edge of the couch and crosses his legs. I notice his toenails are polished a bright pink. They look nice. I pop open a beer and hand it to him.

"You changed your mind about seeing me again... I thought you got all you wanted from me on the beach that day, and, well, you know what they say about buying the goat when you already got the cheese for free?"

I wince because that was certainly direct, and I accept that I hurt his feelings. I probably treated him no differently than he's been treated many times before, but this doesn't make it right. My shame is real, and it owns me; I wait for my mind to start spinning with questions about what I'm doing with a guy who truly needs more than somebody as broken as me for a friend, and then for the world to dim and fade away. But neither happens.

"Look, Vedie, I know you think I took advantage of you that day, but it wasn't...it isn't like that." Before he can say anything, I add, "I've been alone for a long time now, and I just don't think this old dog can learn new tricks."

"You mean you've been playing the field forever, and you don't know if you can be true to one person?" He doesn't hold back on the sarcasm.

"That's not it at all." Although he's challenging me, he's still relaxed and is somehow melting into the arm of the sofa. I'm feeling something with him I can honestly say I've never experienced with any man before: I'm not afraid. He doesn't make me want to run and hide. So I give him a little truth. "I've never had an actual romantic relationship."

"Never? But you're so hot!" His eyes widen, and in an instant, his cynicism is gone.

I smile when I'd normally scowl. "Maybe I'm hot, but I'm also...different. I'm sure you've noticed I have some quirks."

"I've got a couple quirks too, and I'm damn sure you haven't missed *them*." He points to his pink headband and winks.

I grin and he returns it. With no makeup, Vedie looks fresh and young—with a wholesome sort of beauty that appeals to me in a different way than the spirited boyish Vedie or the sexy-lady Vedie. He shifts his weight and molds his body to mine.

And I stay.

Pressed against my chest, he makes me feel strong and brave. And within a few minutes, he's sleeping on my shoulder, his breathing effortless and steady, which seems to prove his trust in a manner more convincing than words. I shake my head a couple times before leaning back, kick my feet up onto the coffee table, and drop my arm around his shoulder.

All of this sweet, heartfelt pleasure is completely new to me. Here I sit, enjoying it so thoroughly—not to mention feeling like something of an imposter. I'm basking in the warm glow of trust I don't deserve.

This is when I come to a shocking realization: I'm looking forward to waking up tomorrow morning. There's nothing I want right now that I don't have. I'm attracted to the person beside me, but not afraid, and my mind hasn't separated from my body. I haven't floated to the ceiling where I can observe our interaction from a safe distance. I'm not lonely. I feel like a man, not a boy.

At this very moment, I might even be...happy.

IT'S VEDIE'S TURN to have nightmares.

He trembles and perspires and begs the tormenter in his dreams to please leave him alone. What shocks me most is I suddenly realize my pain is not unique; Vedie's cries of anguish are too similar to mine to be just another nightmare. He's experiencing a flashback—a different place, time, and persecutor than mine—but in the dark of night, he's reliving his unique pain in the same way I so often relive my own.

Vedie has scars, too. They're just scars I can't see.

Experiencing night terrors, even from the outside looking in, sweeps me back in time. I tried so hard to leave my heart behind in New England when I decided it was time to cut and run to a remote tropical island. And for the past ten years, since I left everyone who meant anything to me on the North Shore of Massachusetts and came to this isolated place, I've worked with diligence to achieve my goal: to feel nothing.

Years ago, I learned that if I can feel happiness and safety and love, I can also feel terrified and anxious and at risk—and very, very angry. I have long considered it a fair trade-off: no feeling good for no feeling bad.

My strategy to live without feelings has worked fairly well. I've been an emotional iceberg since the day I set foot on Placida Island nearly a decade ago. But when I encounter the sleeping expressions of Vedie's distress—his fearful pleadings and the wetness of his tears on my wrist—everything inside me that has been frozen for so long suddenly turns into a huge mound of slush. A dirty, gray slushy New England snowbank, melting on a hot Florida sidewalk.

"You're okay now, Vedie. Joey let you go. I made him let you go," I declare, as if I'm some sort of hero.

His eyes flash open, and although I'm fairly certain he's still technically asleep, there's relief in his expression. He sighs and snuggles against me, so close now he's on my chest. And I feel warm and good.

A very unusual reaction for me.

MATT'S JOURNAL DATED JULY 2008

The ordeal has been over for eight years, and still, I can barely get through several nights without enduring dreams so devastating they drive me straight from deep sleep into a state of agitated hyperalertness.

Nightmares. I can't jump ship from them like I can from the shit I'm not able to deal with during the daytime—by slipping to the safe place behind my eyes. The dreams hit me hard, almost as if they're flashbacks. The horror of Daniel is vivid and more realistic than in my memories. During my years of therapy, I learned this type of nightmare is a symptom of post-traumatic stress disorder, not that the information helps me much.

PTSD. Veterans of war, victims of natural disaster, and nut-jobs like me.

Chapter Six

VEDIE

"The least I can do is cook you a decent breakfast." When Mateo comes into the kitchen, I'm frying eggs in a pan. "After all, you saved my ass last night. And you've done it two times over."

He's naked except for a white towel tied around his waist. His wet hair falls right to his shoulders—still tangled from the shower—and he's giving off this serious Tarzan vibe. He's also sizing me up, probably trying to figure out what kind of mood I'm in today.

"You didn't have to cook, Vedie."

"I'm the kind of person who wants to show how thankful he is. Mama raised me right." That is, until she tossed me out on my ass for being queer.

He sits down at the kitchen table, and I notice the scars on his back for the first time. I gasp, because I know about those kinds of marks. I've got a few of the same sort on the backs of my thighs. They're the kind of scars you earn through hours—or even days—of pain and suffering. They cut deep enough into your skin to scratch the shrunken-up soul inside, making you different than you were before you got them.

Puckered pink ropes of pain written on your skin—that kind of shit changes you.

I don't say anything about them, because who wants to chat over breakfast about shit like getting the skin whipped off your back with a leather belt? Instead, I come over to the table with the frying pan in hand and slide a couple eggs on his plate and then a couple on my own. "Would've made bacon, too, but didn't see any in the fridge. Gimme a sec, and I'll grab the toast."

Once the butter's melting on the toast, I sit across from Mateo, and we eat. I'm starving, but I use my best manners, even dabbing my paper napkin at the corners of my mouth every now and then. After his last bite, Mateo says, "Thank you, Vedie."

"Like I said, it wasn't a problem."

"So, we've got to fix your bicycle tires today." He doesn't look at me when he says it. I want to ask, "What's this 'we' shit?" but I keep my mouth shut.

"I can get it done by myself," I say instead, which is pretty much the same damn thing.

"It'll be much easier if I drive you and your bike to Parsen's Bike Store on the mainland. They'll fix it for you in no time at all."

I can't help it. I snort a little too loud when I pick up our plates. "Yeah, right. I could do that, maybe if the sky opened up and rained down buckets of cash, but not in real life." I take the dishes to the sink and rinse them off.

"I could help with the payment part." The words roll off his lips like a question, but I know it's not one. He gets up, walks right on past where I'm standing at the sink, and into the next room. From there he calls, "I'm settled on the island, and I have no cash flow problems, but you're still trying to get your life here set up. You need to hang on to what money you have."

"I'm no whore. Not gonna fuck you for cash," I mumble. I don't cross my arms and use my bitchy tone because he's in the next room. I say it soft and breathy, filled with breezy, morning air.

He must have damn fine hearing because he replies, "I don't remember asking you to fuck me. We're, uh, we're friends, Vedie." Getting the word friends out of that pretty mouth isn't easy for him. It sounds as if he swallowed something sour and prickly and had to hack it right back up. "And if it makes you feel better, you can pay me back once you're established and have some money to spare."

"I suppose." It sounds reasonable. "So what sort of work you do down here, anyhow? You don't seem too bad off." I stand in front of the mirror in the hallway and twist my loose, damp dreads, one by one. Before Mateo woke up, I helped myself to his shower, but I used the hand towel next to the sink to dry off because I didn't want to go using up his clean towels. Then I stuck on the same borrowed—or stolen—white T-shirt I slept in to cook breakfast.

He again walks past me without grabbing my ass and says, "I blog for businesses. I have a degree in marketing, and it's something I can do from here. And I do some web design. Care for coffee?"

"I'm more into tea, if you've got it."

"I'll make you a cup. Why don't you go get dressed?"

Still thinking about how smart he must be to "blog for businesses," I nod, go grab my pack off the living room floor, and head to the bathroom. My head is full of thoughts about how I'm a dumbass. I don't even have my high school diploma because junior year, the bullying got to be too much, so I quit. And Mr. Hollow Eyes, here, has got himself a college degree. I shake my head knowing we don't have one single thing in common. Plus, there's my new decision that I'm not planning on getting busy with him any time soon.

"Dude's gonna lose interest in me faster than you can say 'Vedie's not giving out free ass or blow jobs.'" Again, I mumble the words out loud, but this time Mateo doesn't hear.

I pull on my short denim cutoffs and a loose and flowy white blouse I bought for two bucks at the thrift shop near the Placida Island Public Library. My dreads look as good as they get, so I leave my hair flying free, but I go to town with makeup. I stick on my fake, jeweled flip-flops, and I'm good to go.

"You look pretty," he tells me when I step out of the bathroom.

"Forgot to stick my dangly earrings in my backpack." As if he gives a shit.

"You still look pretty." He glances away. "Drink your tea, and then we can go pick up your bike and get the tires fixed."

MY BIKE IS in the Parsen's Bike Hospital, or so the bike doctors there call it. We have to kill a couple hours in Windward so they have time to fix it. First, we walk up the narrow main street of the village until we come to a pharmacy, where Mateo picks up some shampoo, body wash, and dish soap, and I grab a tube of dark green mascara.

"Gotta tell ya', Mateo, ain't so sure how I lived without this until now."

He smiles at me real sweet. "It'll look good on your eyelashes."

I think so too.

After shopping, we find a cute little coffee shop and sit to wait for eleven o'clock.

"Have you given any thought to going to the police and reporting Joey for sexual assault?" he asks.

I've got to fight not to laugh. "Cops don't give a shit about freaks like me." I sip my chai latte and add, "They think my sort of people deserve what we get because we're not normal—and, you know, we ask for trouble." I gesture toward my clothes and then my makeup. "You know?"

"I hate that word...normal." Mateo looks the same kind of pissed off as when Joey was groping me last night in the men's room. "I don't think there's only one type of person who's normal."

"You should try being me for a day." Plus, I can't go to the cops; I'm scared shitless that word of where I'm living could get back to folks up in Boston. Hiding makes no sense if the dudes who want to whip your butt until you're straight as an arrow know where you snuck off to. "So, anyhow, now it's my turn for a question, seeing as you asked me one."

There's that flicker in his eyes, and I worry his spirit is going to up and disappear, but it doesn't. Wary, he says, "Well, go ahead and ask."

"Okay." *Here goes nothing.* "Are you gay or straight?"

Again, when his eyes slide off to the side, I'm sure I pushed it too far, and he's going to go hide in that place in the back of his head. And he *does* visit there for a second or two, but he slips right back to the café. "I don't see how it matters."

"It doesn't matter to you? Hmmm, maybe you're bi..."

He shakes his head. "It's just I had my share of troubles as a kid...and I think...I think it left me rather..." He stops talking and clears his throat.

I wait for him to finish, but instead, he does what I've been expecting for a while now—he slips behind his gorgeous eyes, and I might as well be sitting here alone. I reach across the table, grab his hand, and squeeze it so he knows I don't care too much what his answer was going to be anyhow.

"Damned faggot!" A couple of businessmen wearing fancy-ass suits frown at me. And they look as if they might hurl into their coffee cups.

The taller of the two dudes stares right into my eyes. "Why don't you go back to the island of queers where you belong?"

Mateo's hand is still in mine as I stand up to leave. We don't need to get into a café brawl this morning. But he pulls his hand away and sticks it on my shoulder. Then he pushes me back down real gentle.

"Who the fuck are you talking to?" Mateo's back from wherever he went, and he's pissed off. He stands, and shit, is he ever big. I can't exactly stand beside him and look mean and tough when my butt cheeks are peeking out of my booty shorts. But damn, I wish I could. I wish to hell I had on the guy's clothes I left in my backpack in Teo's truck.

"I'm talking to your faggot boyfriend," one of the guys says. They both stand, but they don't look so much like they think their shit don't stink anymore. They actually look kind of puny next to Mateo.

"Say you're sorry."

Oh, my God! What the fuck is Mateo doing? I'm used to getting called names. *Doesn't he know I bring this shit on myself just by how I dress?*

"Mateo, let's leave. I don't need an apology."

It's as if I never said a thing. He keeps on staring them down and demands one more time, "Apologize."

When the two dudes still don't say a word, he gets right in their faces. "Don't you have any manners? Didn't you guys ever learn that if you don't have something nice to say, keep your fucking traps shut tight?" He grabs them by their silky ties, and I swear the smaller one looks like he's about to crap the seat of his fancy pinstriped pants.

"Christ, man, let me go! Look, I didn't mean anything by it." The guy is shaking in his lace-up oxford wingtip shoes, and let me tell you, I would be too, because Mateo looks like he's the pissed-off bodyguard for somebody who matters. "Okay. I'm sorry. Okay?" He looks up at Mateo.

"Say it to him." Mateo glances at me.

"Hey, man..." The guy looks at me. "No hard feelings. I'm sorry for running my mouth." Reluctantly, Mateo releases Mr. Oxford Shoes, who grabs at his collar and yanks at his tie a few times to loosen it, probably because he's close to choking.

"And you?" Mateo's wild eyes shift to the wigged-out guy in penny loafers.

Those loafers would sure look cute with argyle knee socks and a short kilt. I'm big time into shoes.

Mr. Penny Loafers looks directly at me. "Sorry. I was only joking."

Mateo lets him go but glares when he tells him, "It wasn't funny."

The businessmen rush from the café and I want to do the same thing because every eyeball in the joint is glued onto me. Mateo sits back down, all relaxed, as if nothing close to a coffee bar brawl just went down, and he says, "Back to the question you asked when we were interrupted... I'm not gay or straight or bi. In fact, I'm not sure there's a word for what I am. I just know I like you."

There I go, blushing like a schoolboy again.

We hurry up and finish our drinks and head back a little early to the bike hospital. I'm glad to go because we've been getting some chilly glares from the waiter ever since Mateo chased off the suits.

MY BMX IS better than perfect because not only are the tires brand new, but I also got a surprise. My bike's showing off a brand new hot-pink seat with a diamond pattern in the vinyl. I have to do this blink and swallow thing until the wetness in my eyes dries up because Mateo did this sweet thing for me.

MATT'S JOURNAL DATED FEBRUARY 2009

When I was first at Daniel's house, time had no meaning. I more or less survived each day—suffered the beatings, the threats, and the terror—always stopping my brain if it ever dared to consider yesterday or tomorrow. Nighttime was the worst part of my suffering because of the duct tape. He used it liberally—to keep me from both escaping and crying out, not that anyone would have heard my screams in the trailer's remote location.

Daniel worked the night shift as a maintenance man at a nursing home. Anyone would think his absence would have been a short reprieve—a chance for me to breathe easy until he showed up again. But it wasn't, because of what he did to maintain control of me when he was gone. He taped me up. I spent my nights stuck to the legs of the table in the trailer's dirty, cracked-floor kitchen. And with three layers of duct tape wrapped around my head—directly over my mouth on each pass—I was left with two stuffy nostrils to draw in enough air to keep me alive.

Breathing became my singular goal. I obsessed over every single inhalation, all night long. I was actually relieved when Daniel returned from work, because although I knew it was going to be hell with him, it was going to be a living hell.

In hindsight, I think I would have been better off dead than living that way. But the human will—even that of a helpless, broken child—is strong, and I fought to survive each day for reasons I still don't understand.

I'M STILL SEETHING because of the way those two men in the coffee shop treated Vedie. And I'm starting to get the picture. People don't come much better than Vedie, but he doesn't get even a fraction of the respect he deserves. Just because he pays more attention to his feminine side than most guys, he's treated as if he's a mutant of some sort—a suitable depository for people's lust and insults. I hate it that I might also have dismissed him as a "freak show" had I not been so desperate for human interaction on the night we met.

Still fuming, I stop the truck on the street in front of his apartment. He looks over at me and his eyes are wet on the outer edges, but he doesn't try to wipe the wetness away with his wrist. In this way, he's letting me know how he feels, so I push away my anger at the world and face my new friend.

"Thank you for all you've done for me, Teo...ever since things went bad last night."

I nod, not wanting to be thanked in words, but longing for a kiss. On my lips...or on my cheek. I don't much care where. I just want one. As a sign I'm forgiven for the disrespect I showed him and that I'm trusted as a friend... and that he likes me.

And Christ, my last reason is so second grade. The grade I was to be entering at school when Daniel reached into my life and ripped me away from everything I knew.

"I'm gonna grab my bike out of the back of the truck and carry it up the stairs so I can keep it inside my room. Don't want anybody to mess with it again." Vedie goes to open the door, but I'm out and climbing into the bed of the truck before he can blink an eye.

I grab the bike and place it on the ground, and when I'm standing on the street beside it, I sling it over my shoulder. "No worries, I've got it."

His eyes light up and he heads toward the stairs, swinging his hips the whole way, and I can tell he's happy. Simple things such as treating him with basic decency make his day. The iceberg inside me melts some more.

When he gets to the door, though, I notice immediately that the smile drops from his lips, and clouds replace the brightness I've seen in his eyes all afternoon. Nonetheless, he squares his shoulders and pulls a key out of his backpack, then turns around quickly, pressing his back against the door. "Well, it was sure nice to hang out with you. I can...um... You can put my bike down right here, and I'll carry it in after you take off."

Something isn't right. I don't know him like the back of my hand, but I have a pretty good sense there's a problem when his eyes grow dark.

"Unlock the door and step aside, Vedie. I'll carry your bike inside."

He shakes his head and glances away, knowing his honest eyes will give him away.

I place the bike down on the landing, more determined now to see whatever it is he's hiding behind his back. "Here, hold onto your bike." To do so, he'll have to step away from the door.

Again, he shakes his head.

"Vedie, please move out of the way." I plan to look after him if he won't look after himself.

Reluctantly, he steps forward and grasps the handlebars. And that's when I see the sign on the door. Written in bold black print on a torn piece of a cardboard box, taped to the door with a strip of gray duct tape I can barely stand to look at for reasons too painful to recall, is a message.

YOU A DEAD BITCH!

Chapter Seven

VEDIE

"Go in and pack whatever you need. You're coming back to my place and staying until we clear up this problem."

Mateo doesn't need to baby me. "This shit isn't a first for me, man. I've been in this spot before—a dozen times, at least." I wheel my bike forward, unlock the door, and push it open. "I'll be okay."

I suddenly feel ridiculous wearing a stupid flowy blouse. After leaning my bike against the star-covered wall, I go straight to the plastic clothes bin and grab a plain blue T-shirt and some basketball shorts.

"Hang on for a sec." I step behind my open closet door to change. After kicking off my flip-flops that look god-awful with gym shorts, I walk back to Mateo who's now standing in the open doorway, looking kind of badass.

"Pack a bag, Vedie. You're coming with me." I'm faced with a different sort of Mateo than I'm used to. He's super calm, as always, but there's a quality about him that's large and in charge. He's not going to let me mess with him, just like the Mateo in the café didn't take the two assholes' shit. *And* like the Mateo who told me to get my goddamn hand off his shoulder on the night we met.

"Take a chill pill, big dawg. I'm coming." Trying to act cool—as if I'm not scared shitless of Joey, who I'm pretty sure hung the love note on my door—I grab my leopard-print duffel bag. But my stupid shaking fingers don't get with the program, and I drop the bag twice as I carry it to my bed.

"Pack a lot of clothes. I'm not sure how long you're going to be staying." He's firm, almost bossy, and I'm not sure I like it. Or maybe I *really* like it. I'm not too certain of which, at the moment, because I'm still in shock over the scary note.

"I'm not gonna move in with you, Mateo. I'll grab a few different kinds of things, because, you know, my mood changes. But I'm not gonna fill up the back of your truck with my shit." Our eyes meet, and I'm pretty sure he got my message: This is a temporary situation.

I've got my own back. Never had much choice.

I stuff the bag with T-shirts and shorts and some skirts and pretty tops. I pick up my flip-flops off the floor and head to the bathroom to grab my beauty shit because I'm going to want it if I get to feeling softer later on tonight.

"We're going to swim a lot. Take whatever you want to wear in the water."

I know what he's trying to tell me, so I grab my red Speedo briefs *and* my purple plaid bikini.

When my bag is full, he steps over to the bed, grabs ahold of it, and slings it over his shoulder. "Let's go."

MATT'S JOURNAL DATED NOVEMBER 2009

I started disconnecting very early during my time with Daniel.

On the day he grabbed me, he took me straight to his place—a small trailer on a remote wooded lot just over an hour from my home. He stuck me in a narrow, dusty, broom closet and left me there for what seemed to be forever but was probably only one night. There are no words to describe my fear as I huddled in that small dark space.

When he finally dragged me out of the closet, he beat me up. I'd never been so much as spanked by my parents, so a belt to my back and a fist to my face sent a strong message. Then back into the closet I went. A few days of this treatment with little food, or water, and only a small plastic pail in which to piss and shit, and I was putty in his hands. When he dealt me the standard issue, "I know where you live, and if you try anything stupid, I'll go to your house and kill your mother," I had no reason to doubt him.

The first time I disassociated was about four days into captivity when I woke up on the kitchen floor and he was on my back. With only a few swipes of his greasy finger to get me ready, he shoved his dick into me—the physical pain was indescribable, and to be honest, I can feel my awareness slipping away even as I write this. It was that bad. In fact, it was too much for a seven-year-old boy to cope with, and I remember how my entire lower body got numb... I'm pretty sure I somehow made this happen with my mind. And within minutes, I slipped entirely out of the small dazed body on the kitchen floor, trapped beneath the weight of a full-grown man.

THE SOFTER SIDE of Vedie doesn't appear—not when we return to my cottage, not when we swim in the ocean, and not when we grill burgers for supper on the back deck. But it's not a problem for me because I appreciate both sides of him.

Eating burgers and chips, I can't help but stare at his cherry-red Speedo briefs drying on the railing. I think about how we swam together this afternoon. We raced back and forth and dunked each other under the water, and laughed like a couple of kids. Yeah, Matthew North, former abducted and abused child, laughed so hard that peach iced tea shot out of his nose.

"Fun day, man," Vedie says, and I can tell by the question in his eyes he wants me to reassure him I had fun too.

So I'm honest with him. "Can't remember a better one."

He folds his arms across his chest, and I recognize the defiant body language. "Better than the day I gave you a blow job on the beach?"

I choke on the bite of burger I'm chewing, but I don't slip away.

"Well...was today better than that day, Mateo?" He's daring me to say the wrong thing. In fact, I think he's testing to see if I prefer his feminine or masculine side.

"Is...uh...there only one correct answer? Because both days worked well for me." A diplomatic answer.

He stands up, steps over to the railing, and runs his fingertips over the damp Speedo. He's only wearing a pair of black basketball shorts, and I find myself studying his slim, curved brown back and slumped shoulders that resemble those of a laid-back teenage boy. "Just answer, Mateo." He stays still as a statue except for a slight shudder when a breeze blows off the water.

"Today was better."

With puzzled eyes, he turns toward me. "You don't like me when I'm girlish?" He covers his mouth with his hands, and I know he's stunned and shocked and scared.

"I like every part of you."

"But how could you get into horsing around with me better than me getting you off?"

I never cry, but if I did, I'd do it now. Vedie has no idea of his human worth, which brings to mind the years when I was Daniel's...and I felt like nothing. So I decide to make him understand. "It's because we had fun and..." *And sure, I liked touching you and feeling good. A lot. You're sexy and you took me to heaven with your mouth, I won't lie.* "And it's just...getting to know you... To me, it's better."

I think I actually came out and told Vedie way too much truth for comfort. I'm about to turn away from him and am taken by surprise when he dives into my arms. He doesn't say anything as he clings to me. He doesn't need to. I pull him tight to my chest, and I like the way he holds me right back, not sweet and soft the way he did that day on the beach, but hard and rough like he's a guy in need. And even when my instinct is to shove him away—because nobody grabs me, ever—I let him hold on, and I honestly don't want him to let go.

I have no clue what is happening to my solitary life.

VEDIE

For a very long time, me and Mateo stand on the porch, stuck together like we're glued. So long we get kind of sweaty even though there's a good breeze blowing off the water.

"Are you ready for bed yet, Vedie?"

I hear the word bed, and I get an urge to head off to the bathroom and make a change. So I nod and walk to the kitchen where I dropped my duffel bag, and drag it to the bathroom. Usually, my softer self shows up before I get busy with a dude. But not today.

I've always known I was male, and I never wanted to call myself anything else. But back in middle school, I figured out there's a part of me that feels female. And I always knew which side of Vedie needed to show up and when. Say, if I was at school or work, I was always boyish, and that meant no makeup, no skirts, and no soft voice. I guess I thought I could deal with people's bullshit better when I was looking at the world through a boy's eyes, plus, I could fight better in guys' clothes. And I had to fight a lot back then.

Growing up, I only let my girlish side out when I felt safe. Like when I babysat my little cousins, Dara and Rico, I let the softer side of me show because it worked real good for all three of us. But after all the shit that's been going down with Joey lately, it's as if the fear is sticking to me. I don't feel soft, and I don't feel sweet. I feel scared and pissed off and... I just can't lie back and let a man take me, even if Mateo's the man.

"You okay in there, Vedie?" Mateo calls through the bathroom door. Shit. I've been standing here gawking at myself in the mirror for ten minutes. Teo probably thinks I fell in the toilet bowl. I flush to buy some time.

"Um...yeah...just washing up." I pull down my shorts and briefs and step out of them. Using a washcloth I find beside the sink and the liquid hand soap, I wash up real quick and then grab my bottle of perfume from the bottom of my bag. But I stop myself before I start spraying. I'm just not feeling it tonight. "Be right out, Teo."

"Okay."

I grab a lacey hair band and wrap it around my head and look in the mirror. The face looking back at me is pretty enough to pass as a girl's, even without makeup. I don't have a man's thick brow or a chin that looks strong. I've got wide eyes and a pointed chin and full lips. Girly. But still, I'm not feeling it tonight.

After brushing my teeth, I grab a tank top and my one pair of plain white boxers and pull them on. Then I stick my bag in the corner and leave the bathroom, but my head's not in the right space for what I figure Mateo's going to want to do.

Mateo's waiting for me in the hall. He got changed while I was in the bathroom. And he only sleeps in snug black boxer briefs. *Yum*, I think, even though I'm not in the mood. And I can tell he's surprised when he looks at me and sees all-boy. I'm kind of surprised too.

"I'm not gonna fuck you." I cross my arms and throw out my hip the way a ticked off teenage girl would do if her mama said her shorts were too short and she wasn't going out in public dressed like that. I speak in a hard voice because I'm not the sweet Vedie right now. I'm actually not sure who I am, besides a hot mess.

"I never said I wanted to fuck you," he sneers and, out of the corner of his mouth, adds, "Don't flatter yourself."

"That was mean!" I yell into his face. I'm ready for him to be nasty to me and...it's as if I'm nothing but a confused balloon and Mateo stuck me with a pin and all of the air is fizzling out of me. I sink to the floor.

Mateo doesn't want me when I'm not all soft and pretty. He doesn't want me.

"Damn it, Vedie." He squats and pulls me real rough against his chest. I want to push him away and tell him to shove off, but it feels too sweet in his arms. His voice gets low and quiet, like he's letting me in on some big secret. "I get mad when you act as if I'm going to force you to...to have sex with me. It's not my way. I wouldn't do that to you."

I try to stay cool—I almost never cry when I'm feeling manly. "I know you ain't gonna rape me!" One deep breath, and the rest of the shit in my brain spills out. "I say stuff like that because I know if you don't try anything on me, I won't give it all up to you!"

I stand, but he doesn't let go. He gets up with me and pushes me back by my shoulders, just far enough so he can see my face. And shit, if he's not grinning. "I tempt you, Vedie—is that what you're saying?"

"Well, yeah! Have you checked out your pecs in the mirror lately? They're friggin' tempting as hell! I've gotta try hard not to drool!"

He releases this huge snort—like a spurt of laughter got stuck in his throat and escaped out of his nose.

"Are you laughing at me?" Now I'm pissed off.

One big paw comes up to cover his mouth. He shakes his head and mumbles, "No, sir." And that's nothing but bullcrap—I know laughing lips when I see them.

"What's so friggin' funny, huh?" I'm getting madder by the second.

"You...you're so...so damned cute!"

And when he pulls me against his strong chest and hugs me tight, then kisses my cheek as if I'm something special, I stand perfectly still because I suspect the softer side of me is going to pop right out. But she doesn't.

"Let's go to bed, Vedie. And don't worry, I promise your virtue is safe with me." I can still hear the smile in his voice.

I ain't so sure your virtue is safe with me, Mateo, I think, but keep it to myself. I lay a quick, wet kiss on his lips, and he stumbles before heading down the hall.

MATT

Vedie is an enthusiastic cuddler. So enthusiastic that at first, I'm not sure if I'll be able to sleep with him. But damn, he looks hot in his snug white boxers and skimpy tank top—slim, but still strong. No gloss shines on his lips and no charcoal lines are drawn around his eyes. Tonight, he looks more like a guy I might see at a gym or a bar. And I appreciate his manliness—the outline of his pecs and his dick through thin cotton entice me more than I expect. And the bonus is I can't find it in my heart to feel even slightly intimidated by him.

He's wrapped around me now. I'm actually shocked I can tolerate the sensation of his smooth legs entwined with mine, his nest of sweet-smelling dreads right under my nose, and his short fingernails raking eagerly through the hair on my chest, but I'm still here and liking it. And the strangest part of this scene is I'm wondering about him—I want to know why he left his home up north and who he's trying so hard to hide from.

His sigh is noisy and distinct, a sound I'm meant to hear. "You wanna know who threw me out like trash so I landed down here all alone, don't you?" His tone is honest, not teasing. I wonder how he knows I want to hear his story, which is so uncharacteristic of me. Sometimes I think he can read my thoughts.

"Sure...I'd love to know who I can call to thank for your presence on this lonely island," I reply.

"Ha! You think you're so funny, don't you?" He leans up on his elbow, and I can see two points of light in his eyes, a reflection from the moon shining in the bedroom window. Suddenly, he's serious. "You can't call anybody, Teo. Because I'm in hiding."

This guy is pretty much an open book—doesn't he know people in hiding keep it to themselves? I can't suppress a shiver of fear for him. Thinking I'm cold, he reaches down and pulls the sheet up over my shoulders and then tucks it in.

"So nobody knows you're here?"

"Uh-uh. At least I hope not."

"Why are you in hiding?"

He doesn't hesitate to answer. "You've seen me at my finest, Teo...a frilly skirt and a clingy top, with pretty makeup and hair that smells all flowery. Add to this picture of me a nice pair of five-inch shiny black patent leather pumps with ankle straps and—"

"I get your point—you like to wear women's clothing." I fail to see where he's going with this.

"Well, a dude can't get by dressed that way where I come from. At least not a dude like me who doesn't know his way around a switchblade."

And it's suddenly crystal clear—he couldn't publicly express his femininity if he stayed at home where people know him and have traditional expectations of him as a man. "I see."

"Mama said to me, 'I knew you were one of those queers since you were four years old, but Vedie, you're a freak of nature when you dress up in those lady's clothes. I don't know *what* you are, so you're gonna have to get gone!'"

"I'm sorry." Vedie was thrown out of his house because he couldn't fit in. I ran away from mine for the same reason. We're opposite sides of the same coin.

"No need to be sorry for me, but if I stayed up there in the city, I was gonna live to regret it. Or maybe just plain not live. See, my brothers, Tyrone and Marcus, and my cousin James, thought they could change me—make me want *girls* the way they do and stop me from wanting to wear *girls' clothes* so much." He's quiet for a second, and this time, he shudders. "They gave it a damn good shot, too, plenty of times."

His voice trembles, and the sound cuts me deep inside. I understand that the efforts those guys made to change him likely weren't much fun.

"But Mateo, I can't change it." He untangles his legs from mine and flops flat on the bed. "I'm into cross-dressing. That's what it's called, you know, when I dress in clothes the world thinks are meant for women." He speaks as if he's reciting words from a textbook, slowly and clearly. "I'm a guy, and I'm fine with the body I've got, but sometimes, I wanna be the way I see girls as being. I wanna wear pretty clothes, and be soft and sweet, and maybe even cry, if it's how I feel." I already miss the way his ankles hooked around mine, but I focus on my need to grasp how he expresses his gender. "I know I can't be how *all* women act because there is no 'all' when it comes to people. But I can't make any of this stuff fit in my life when I live in Boston."

"I think I get it." I understand what he just told me, but I don't get how he found the courage to share his personal information with me. I could never open up in this way.

"Mostly, nobody in my neighborhood got it. You ever met somebody like me before?"

"If I did, they didn't explain it."

"Well, I think maybe part of me is broken, Mateo. I'm not supposed to follow rules for both boys and girls, but I do. And this part of me can't be fixed—believe me, my brothers and cousins tried."

It's funny, but I don't see Vedie as in need of fixing. All he needs is to be accepted. "You're not broken."

He ignores my statement. "Lots of people like me feel as if they've got to hide how they are. But not me...not anymore, at least. I'm all done with hiding."

It doesn't seem to occur to Vedie that he's still living his life in hiding from his family. He simply focuses on how he's expressing his gender honestly in his life on Placida Island. We're both quiet for a few minutes, and then I ask my last pressing question. "What happens if they find out where you are? You know, your brothers and cousin and friends?"

"I hope to hell they don't. But if they do, I hope they don't give a shit about me anymore."

I sincerely hope Vedie's family and friends don't come looking for him because I know people don't lose their prejudices easily.

"Mateo, me and you, we've got something major in common." He snuggles up against my side. "Don't talk. Just think over what I'm about to say. Okay?"

"Okay."

"I think you and me have got more than one soul living inside us. I've got my boy-self and my girl-self living in me. You've met both of them." He's quiet for a second. "And you've got strong, brave Mateo...and scared shitless Mateo. I wanna get to know both of the souls who live in you."

He leans up on one elbow and studies my face in the dim light. I'm not one to stare, but his skin is so smooth and beautiful, I can't look away. Soon, he drops down and snuggles against me again, letting his fingers take over the exploration. He traces the line of hair on my chest down to my belly, and then down some more to find my dick. When he wraps his fingers around me, I have to resist the urge to roll away—not because it doesn't feel like the promise of heaven, but because it brings to mind darker days. But when he leans over and kisses me, I'm distracted from everything by his soft lips.

"Let me take care of you tonight, Mateo." His mouth moves against the stubbly side of my face, and his voice is so raspy and deep I know his urge to please me comes from deep within the masculine part of his soul.

When I nod, he begins to stroke. And I give up all control to the man beside me, who mumbles assurances about how I shouldn't worry because he's in charge here. When I stiffen before I come, he urges, "That's good, Mateo. Give it to me and I'll keep it safe." He could never know how much those words mean to me.

With his hand damp from my release, he turns his attention to his own dick, and we rock together as he takes care of himself. I feel guilty because, as far as bringing him pleasure, I've been passive. But he doesn't seem to think I left him stranded. After he comes, he pins me beneath him for the longest and deepest kiss I've ever shared.

And then, after an extended sigh, he flops onto my chest and fades away into sleep, leaving me behind to consider what he said and what I let him do.

Chapter Eight

MATT'S JOURNAL DATED APRIL 2010

At Daniel's house, I learned quickly to keep calm at all costs.

In the beginning, I had no idea how to soothe myself. Before, soothing Matthew was exclusively Mommy's job. In one horrible moment, times had completely changed, and now, neglect and rape were the extent of my primary human relationship. Daniel only spoke to me when he needed to dictate to "Mark" the rules of the house, remind me to call him "Dad" in public, and yell at me for screwing up. Nurturing and love? Um…not in my world.

So what was a kid to do? I made a plan and stuck by it. I refused to allow myself to get too afraid, too angry, too bitter, too lonely, too anything. I blocked all intense emotions. My biggest fear was of feeling afraid. Being deathly scared of fear itself, I focused on staying perfectly calm at all times. This way, I didn't have to sink into despair.

It didn't take long until I'd become a newly crisp autumn leaf, separated from my tree too soon by a forceful tug, even while I was still fresh and green. My days were spent drifting around haphazardly in the wind, unable to resist being pulled up and down, this way and that. I fluttered, without a fight, in the direction of the wind, always aware I was just one breath away from falling to the earth to wither and disintegrate. Like I'd never existed at all.

VEDIE

"I didn't mean to put him on Angie's shit list, Sheila." I'm not exactly living in fear that Joey's going to try and get back at me for what went down the other night, but I know I've got to be on guard. Which is nothing new. I've been living my life on guard since the first time I got called "sissy" in kindergarten.

"It wasn't your decision to give him a written warning, Vedie. When I told Angie how he's always lusting over you, she said she didn't need a sexual harassment lawsuit, so she had to do what she had to do." Sheila's face, shoulders, and arms are bright red from spending the entire day in the sun. She never learns that platinum blondes, even if the color comes from a bottle, need number-fifty sunscreen. "And it's only a warning. It's not as if he got fired."

"Well, he's pissed off at me like you wouldn't believe. Blames my ass for being too hot. You know, as if he couldn't help himself and *had* to feel me up." I stuff as many napkins as will fit on the long, narrow shelf while Sheila fills the ketchups. "When Mateo dropped me off today, Joey was standing out by the bike rack. He shouted, 'Your fine ass don't belong in no men's bathroom, Wilson, making it so the real men in there can't piss straight! Not my fault I grabbed ya.'"

"Well, Angie also told me she's going to designate the single stall bathroom way over by the sand volleyball court as a gender-neutral one. You can use it in private and not have to worry about assholes like Joey anymore."

"Cool." It's way more than cool. The thought that my boss would accommodate what I need makes me misty, but work isn't the time or place for tears, so I blink them back.

"Hey, Vedie...you got a customer on table seven." We both glance toward the beach and see Mateo leaning back in his chair, looking out over the water. "Someday, you've got to tell me how you managed to snag him. Gay guys and straight women of all ages, shapes, sizes, and colors have tried to get with Crazy Matt because he's the hottest guy on the island. And sweet little Vedie, you've been the only one to get anywhere with him." Sheila elbows me. "WTG."

"We're only friends." I wonder if what I just said is true as I pat down my hair, straighten my apron, and head over to where Mateo is waiting.

When I get to his table, I drop a menu on it and ask, "Hey, big dawg, what're you drinking tonight?"

"How about if you choose a beer on tap for me."

"You trust me?"

Those gorgeous eyes get wide, and he blinks. But then he nods.

"Good answer. I'll be right back with your brew...and pretty Miss Sheila is gonna be your server tonight." I'm off to the bar, feeling good about shit, for the most part.

THE NIGHT DRAGS on and on, mostly because I know Mateo is waiting for me in his seat at table seven down by the beach. Weird thing is, he doesn't seem to have any problem with waiting. When he finishes eating dinner, he tilts his chair toward the water and nurses a second beer. It's as if he's been made to wait before and he knows how to do it real good.

When I pass by his table, he doesn't try and grab my ass or even talk to me—he doesn't even seem to notice me, but I'm cool with it.

From her spot at the bar, Angie waves me over, and I jog up the beach. "Hey, Vedie. You mind if I let you out early tonight at, say, nine or so? The place couldn't be more dead." It's a slow night, and we both know tips are going to suck.

I glance down the beach at Mateo, visible in the darkness only because he's sitting near a tiki torch. And I do a double take because it looks like an old man and lady are standing by his table, talking to him. "I haven't got a problem with cutting out early, Angie."

"Well, then, go bring drinks to the two new diners at table seven, see if Sheila needs any help with closing down her station, and you can head home." Angie's an all-business lady. She works in a friggin' tiki hut bar and wears a business suit every day, which tells the whole story. She's not too friendly, but she's fair with hours and gives me more respect than I ever got at a job before, so I'm cool with her.

"Sounds like a plan." I'm curious about the people who are now sitting with Mateo. He exchanges a word or two with the workers, but I've never seen him mix it up with other guests. I head down the beach, go right to his table, and hand each of the older people a menu. "Hey, there, folks. My name's Vedie, and I'm here to bring you whatever you want to drink."

The old folks look uncomfortable, almost as if they wish they weren't sitting with Mateo, which is weird as fuck seeing as they asked if they could sit here.

"Thank you, young man," says the old dude, his eyes on Mateo. "Could you get a glass of sweet iced tea for my wife and a diet cola for me?"

"Of course." I glance at Mateo and see Crazy Matt. Truth is, I haven't seen him in a while, and I can't say I missed him too much. His eyes are a strange bronze color in the light of the tiki torch, and they're bugging right out of his head. The dude's ready to cut and run. "Yo, Mateo, how about one more beer?"

The old man and lady look at each other when I call him Mateo. But he nods, super eager, and asks, "When are you off work?"

I look right at the old folks and give them my best smile to cover for Mateo, who's acting kind of rude—almost ignoring them—not that anybody asked for my opinion. "As soon as I bring your drinks, I'm off the clock. But take your time with your friends, here. I can wait for you at the bar."

The man and lady are now gawking at me as if I'm dressed to kill in a tight leather miniskirt that shows off my ass cheeks, a cheetah-print half top, and six-inch stilettos, even though I'm just wearing my work clothes.

"Join us." It comes out sharp, like a demand. And I'm not too used to Mateo ordering me around. But then he adds in a sweeter voice, "Please, Vedie, let me buy you a bite to eat." And the way he says it makes him sound like he's lost all control, plus the empty look in his eyes, tells me he's about to go. As in, leave the restaurant and go to that place in his head where he hides.

"Uh...yeah, sure, I'd love to because I'm starving, but first, can you stop by the bar for a second? Angie's got a question for you about your credit card." I'm not the world's best bullshitter, and the thing is, Mateo always pays in cash. But I've got to talk to him alone, and it's the best I can come up with on the fly.

Mateo looks confused, but it works to bring him back. "I guess so...sure." He looks at the couple who're now gawking at him like he's got three heads and one of them has the face of a pit bull puppy. "Mom, Dad. I'll be right back."

Mom and Dad? What the fuck?

At the bar, I find a shadowy corner and drag his ass there with me. "Mateo, those two old folks are your parents?"

He slides down the side of the wall until he's sitting on his ass in the dirt. He looks up at me, and in a split second, his eyes go blank and his lips start moving.

"Hey, man. You can't zone out right now. Ya hear me?"

His lips keep moving. His eyes are still dull. He's pretty much gone.

So I kneel beside him in the dirt. "Mateo," I say real gentle, "your folks are here, so you gotta come back. I'm not too sure what the hell's going on, but hear this—you aren't alone. I'm gonna get you through this."

He blinks. But nope. He still isn't back here on the ship he just jumped off.

"You've been walking beside me in my troubles with Joey. And you've done a good job by me, man. Real good—better than anybody's ever done by me before, in fact." I place my hand on his shoulder, and he jumps about a mile and a half. "Let's you and me go back to the table and eat some Tiki Hut food with your folks."

Mateo blinks twice, swallows hard, and when his eyes bug out, I know he's back. "I can't do this. I've got to go back to the cottage." His forehead wrinkles up, and his mouth forms a thin straight line. He's panicking—I know the look because I've been up shit creek myself a time or ten.

"Is that what you really wanna do, Teo? Because I'll cut and run with you if it's what you want. But don't you think it might be better if we go back out there, sit down with your folks, talk to them some, and let them know everything's cool with you?"

He shrugs. "Uh...everything's not cool with me."

"So we'll say you and me are best buds? And I'll do lots of talking so they can't ask you too many questions."

Now he shakes his head. "We have to say we're boyfriends. I'll slip away unless I can squeeze your hand."

"Hmmm...are you out with your family?"

The man shrugs again. "They won't care...they'll be...they'll be fucking stunned I let someone into my life." He stops talking and looks at me all serious. "*I'm* fucking stunned I let someone into my life."

This guy might be more a piece of work than I figured. "Okay, let's go do this. Follow my lead."

I stand and pull him to his feet. Mateo's right on the hairy edge of losing it. I wink at him, but all he does is gulp super loud, so I take his hand. Together, we somehow get our asses back to the table.

I swear their eyes are going to pop out of their heads when we come back holding hands. I figure I'll start up our little chat, seeing as Mateo and his parents are friggin' speechless. "So, you're Mr. and Mrs. North, right?"

They look at each other and then back at me. Mr. North finally says, "Yes, we are." He doesn't reach out to shake my hand, but I'm cool with it. Not a biggie.

Sheila brings our drinks, as I managed to let her know I needed this huge favor, and she sticks them down in front of us with a smile. I lift up my beer. "Here's to us having a couple of cold drinks and a bite to eat, and getting to know each other, huh?"

Mrs. North is one of those ladies with a true classy style I only dream of having. In her flowery pink-and-green dress, white ballet flats without no scuff marks, and blunt cut grayish-blonde hair, she looks as if she might be late for a cruise to Bermuda. Mr. North is like an older Mateo. The dude's hair isn't too gray and it's cut short and neat as if he's running for president. His eyes are mostly the same color as his son's, just a few shades darker to make them less stunning. And the man has a thing for whales, it seems, because he's got them all over his shorts and on his belt too. I almost say, "So you're big time into whales, man... You oughta meet my second cousin Shondra, back in the neighborhood, seeing as she's got herself one hell of a collection of plastic killer whales," but I change my mind at the last second.

Mateo lifts his beer to touch it against mine, real obedient, but he doesn't look up. Mr. and Mrs. North sit here all baffled, and finally, Mr. North picks up his soda and nudges his wife, so she picks up her iced tea. We all clink our drinks together, but I wouldn't call it a joyful moment.

"Matt said your name is Vedie. What an odd name..."

Hello, Mrs. Classy! That isn't exactly a polite way to start our little chat. But I'll work with it for Mateo's sake.

"My mama once told me Vedie means 'sight.' And mine's twenty-twenty. *Ha!*" I smile wide. It sucks that nobody else does.

"And you two are...going together?" Mrs. North has the look of a cat that swallowed a hairball and needs to gag it up ASAP.

We all look at Mateo, because this part is his ballgame. " Yes...Vedie's my boyfriend."

His parents turn and look at each other again, and when Mrs. North nods like she's thinking *tell me another one*, I know they're not buying what we're selling.

So I figure I'll sell it better—it's the least I can do for Mateo, and it doesn't require any real sacrifice on my part. I pull my chair right up to his. The warmth of his arm feels good against the back of my hand, and I decide real quick I enjoy faking that we're boyfriends. I lean up against his shoulder, and he stiffens for a second because he isn't used to anybody touching him in public, but he knows me pretty good and trusts me enough, and soon calms down.

"How did you two meet?" Mrs. N asks, then wrinkles up her nose and sniffs as if she's smelling something nasty.

I sniff too, but the air doesn't smell funky, like the toilets are on the blink. So I answer the question because it's as easy as *who's your mother?* I say, "Me and him met right on this very beach, seeing as I work as a busboy here." I put my hand on top of Mateo's, and he turns his up so he can hang on to me.

"Well, Matt, it's good to see you finally have a friend. I wasn't sure we'd ever see the day," his Dad says, and this time, I don't buy what *he's* selling. I think he'd rather see Mateo alone than with the likes of me.

Mateo corrects him. "Boyfriend—we're boyfriends, Dad."

His parents look at each other, and their eyebrows go up—they're more than a little uncomfortable. "So you're gay now, Matthew?" his mother finally asks.

I'm not sure if she's bent out of shape because of the gay thing, or because I'm black, or because it's clear I don't come from the same side of the tracks they live on.

Mr. North clears his throat and looks at me. "So, Vedie, tell us, where are you from? I think I detect a touch of Boston in your accent."

"You've got a good ear, big dawg." I send him one of my friendliest winks, but I don't think he likes it much. He squirms in his seat like he's sitting on a sea urchin.

Mrs. N doesn't give me a chance to answer his question seeing as she's got other shit on her mind. And she doesn't look nearly as pretty with a scowl on her face. "This boy must be fifteen years old. *Really*, Matthew?"

I squeeze Mateo's hand because I think he might be slipping away from our table on the beach. "Excuse me, ma'am, but I'm not fifteen. I've just got some super good face cream that hides the years. If you want, I'll let you borrow a jar for your wrinkles." I send her a wink, too, but I'd bet my fine ass she likes it less than her husband did. "Anyhow, I'm twenty-one."

"That is a profound relief." She makes the I'm-smelling-shit face again.

Reacting to his Mom's words, Mateo's hand slips from mine, and lands on his lap. I look quick to the side and see his eyes are half-closed, which ain't a good sign. "Anyhow, Mateo didn't mention you guys were coming to visit."

"Why? If you knew we were coming, would you have baked a cake?" She asks me, haughty as hell.

Part of the way I live my life now is I don't take crap from anybody, so I play Mrs. N's game. "Yes, ma'am. That's just exactly what I'd do. I think I'd bake you a nice red velvet with a fluffy cream cheese frosting."

Mateo laughs out loud. It seems to come from out of nowhere, because I honestly thought he wasn't paying attention to our little chat. But the sound of his laughter is perfect and right, so I do what comes natural. I lift my head up and kiss his scruffy cheek, and soon as I do it, this fake moment becomes real. He turns my way and looks down into my eyes, and we connect with a silent zing. He's here with me, and he knows I've got his back, just like he's got mine.

And we get frozen, gazing into each other's eyes.

Mr. North clears his throat, and it brings us back to The Only Tiki Hut real fast. When I glance at him, I see he now buys that me and Mateo are big-time in love. And even though he doesn't look exactly thrilled, he can deal with it. Mrs. N is another story, though. She also buys our little act, but I get a feeling she's disgusted because of the way she drops her head in her hands, elbows on the table even, and sighs real loud.

This is when Sheila comes back to the table. "You all up for some food? The kitchen's only open for a few more minutes, and I need to put your order in."

Mrs. N quickly replies, "No, we can't stay. We still have some driving to do tonight and Robert wants to get right back on the road."

Robert North appears as if he could go for a half-pound burger cooked rare and a huge pile of fries, but he doesn't argue with her. "Yes, I suppose Lily's right. We should be going."

"It was nice to meet you both." I use my best manners.

"I'm sure," Mrs. North replies.

Me and Mateo stand, and this time when I look at him, he seems a little pissed off. He says in a cool voice, "I'm so glad you stopped by and had a chance to meet my boyfriend."

This time, I'm not sure if they buy it, but the part they don't buy is that Mateo's glad they stopped by. He doesn't look "so glad" at all.

For the space of a minute, we all stand there gawking at each other. And then, without any hugs or kisses, we say these lame-ass goodbyes, and the North's walk out of The Only Tiki Hut real stiff, like they got two big sticks stuck up each of their tight butts.

Matt grabs his wallet and pulls out a hefty pile of cash that'll way more than cover his dinner and our drinks. He drops the money onto the table, and what he does next damn near floors me. He takes my hand in his and leads me from the restaurant to his truck. I almost forget to worry that Joey might be lurking around the parking lot waiting to beat on my ass.

MATT

Vedie's been to the bathroom and changed into a pretty pink shift, which is a signal he's in a softer mood. We're sitting on the couch, talking about how my parents ended up at The Only Tiki Hut while he eats a strawberry yogurt for dinner.

"Mom and Dad told me they stopped by here, and since I wasn't home, they figured I was at the Tiki Hut."

"Why would they figure you'd be there?" The way he's licking his spoon is making me think about his mouth...and remember that day on the beach. I'm hard as a rock. I blow out a mouthful of air and try to keep my thoughts straight.

"When they drive to the Keys for vacation, they always stop here to see me. They've been doing it for years. And they know the only place I go at night is to the Tiki Hut, so they assumed they'd find me there."

Vedie nods and licks the yogurt off the spoon. "You think they bought that we're a couple?"

I nod and get a little bit harder. "I almost bought it."

He giggles. "Me too."

We sit in awkward silence, and my thoughts start racing because so many wishes and fantasies and fears are passing through my mind. As always, my lips start moving as I recite my thoughts silently.

"Say them out loud." Vedie's voice is light and airy, but somehow also firm.

"Say what?"

"The words on your lips...the words in your head." Vedie leans to place the empty yogurt cup on the coffee table, and a strap of his nightie slips over his shoulder.

I suck in my breath at the sight and offer him the truth. "I don't think you'd approve of everything I'm saying to myself. You aren't that kind of guy."

His sweet smile tells me he appreciates what I just said. He's touched by any small show of respect.

"No. Not anymore, I'm not." He curls his long legs beneath him. "But I promise I won't kick your ass if you tell me the thoughts in your head."

"You promise not *to try* to kick my ass."

He continues smiling, so I close my eyes and allow my voice to fill in the silent, racing notions in my brain.

"I like that you've got characteristics of a man and a woman. I feel comfortable with your male part. I've never had a friendship before...somebody to joke around and act like we're kids. And it's important, I think. But I appreciate the other side of you because sometimes I want your softness...and the sweetness."

My breathing is suddenly strained; I wish I could take back my candid confession. I have no idea why I'm still here and aware. Finally, I open my eyes to see if Vedie's staring at me in horror, but what I see in his eyes is better even than what I saw at the restaurant tonight after he kissed my cheek in front of my parents. His aqua eyes are round and wide and wet and looking at me as if I saved him again.

"Don't stop talking," he urges.

Maybe I'm a fool, but I close my eyes again and leap off the cliff. "I like the curve of your back when you're boyish, and your skinny shoulders and the way your arms aren't ripped but are wiry and strong. And when you're girlish, I like the way your voice gets soft and your eyes get wet, and I want to touch you. But at the same time, I don't want the boy side of you to be completely gone...because Vedie, I'm pretty sure I want both parts of you." I wait to get rebuked for offering honesty I don't even understand, but it doesn't happen.

This time when I open my eyes, Vedie stands, takes my hand, and leads me to the bedroom. We lie down on our sides so we're facing each other, and he asks more bluntly than I expect, "You got a rubber?"

I nod because the last time I went to the store, I let my dream of being intimate with him win out, and I stuck a package of condoms in my grocery pile.

"I've gotta ask one more question, Mateo."

"Of course."

"After we do it, are you gonna dump me off at my apartment and leave me there alone, the way you did before?"

I answer quickly. "No...I couldn't do that."

"Why not?"

"Because...I think...I think it would hurt too much."

It's dark in my room, but I can still see his Mona Lisa smile. I have once again supplied the correct answer, and at the critical moment; my reward will be this unique person's physical affection.

"Make love to me, Teo." He climbs onto my bed, and I follow him. We don't even push the covers back.

When our gazes collide, my heart is filled with a devastating pleasure-pain. I focus on the pleasure and reach for his nightgown, and then pull it swiftly over his head.

I can't help myself; as soon as he's naked, I run my hands all over his chest and finger his nipples like a little boy with a shiny new toy. I'm *too* hungry for him and my effort lacks all finesse, but at the same time, I'm sure he doesn't mind, as he's moaning and twisting beside me on the bed. Before I go on, I pull off my T-shirt and rip down my jeans and briefs, as I won't want to waste time doing this later. We embrace—his body is pressed against mine, from his chest to his toes. His dick presses with purpose against my thigh; he wants me as much as I want him.

"I've gotta slow down, Vedie...or it'll be over too quickly." I lift my body with my arms so I'm hovering above him. I wait as long as I can before slowly bowing my neck to let my mouth play with his. In our very first kiss, I'm taken aback by the enticing fullness of his lips and can't resist the urge to suck his lower one into my mouth and bite it gently.

Daniel used to bite me...for real. I push the cruel thought away and lower my body. Vedie squirms beneath me, but he doesn't push me away. I'm the one calling the shots.

When I've eased my desire for the taste of his lips, I lower my mouth to his jaw and soon to his neck, wondering all the while how a man can taste so sweet. I trace the line of his throat with my tongue, noting how sparse the stubble is on his bronze skin. My fingers return to his chest that is equally free of hair, and although he gasps and twists and squirms, I pinch the tiny buds there to let him know I'm in charge.

"All you need to do is breathe," I inform him in a raspy tone, and he settles back down.

Within a few seconds, I'm sucking on his chest and soon licking his belly. But he interrupts the passionate moment. "You don't have to go down on me, Teo." We both know the next step on my mouth's journey down his body is to his most private area. "Let *me* go down on you."

"I want to taste you." It's a simple statement of fact, to which he only shrugs. I crawl between his silky legs.

He separates them willingly, using one hand to tentatively feed me his dick. With his other hand, he smooths my hair from my face, and when my mouth encloses him fully in its warmth, he utters, "I...I...shit. I've never felt this before. I've only...done it for others."

No man has ever taken him to this place in heaven.

I'm so glad it's me on this new journey with him that I have to stifle an atypical urge to grin, which would make sucking him a challenge. But a few seconds later, I pull off. "Stop me before you come—I want you to come when I'm inside you."

I take my time, my hands and mouth working together to give him as much pleasure as I know how, and when his hips start to move in short choppy thrusts, it's clear the time has come for me to change tactics. I'm about to experience a first, too—as a top with a man. I do my best to ignore his protests when I slide my mouth from him, and I quickly get onto my knees, lean over, and snatch a condom from the drawer in my bedside table. My fingers shake as I unwrap it, but I manage to hastily pull it on. After steadying myself with a single deep breath, I ask, "Do you want to be on your belly? Or can I lift your legs so we can be face-to-face?"

He gasps and nods, and somehow, I know what he wants.

"I need to get you ready so I don't hurt you." I grope around the bed for the lube I dropped when I retrieved the condom. I find it and squeeze a fair amount onto my fingers and insert them inside him, one and then another and soon another.

Daniel never showed me this courtesy.

Vedie's eyes are now tightly shut, and a needy sound escapes from between his lips; he's ready. I prop his ass on my leg for a breathtaking moment and contemplate what I'm about to do. I can't make love to him until I see his eyes and know he's here with me in every way.

Another courtesy Daniel never extended.

I poke his side with one finger and when he opens his eyes, I smile because I can see he is so very with me. "Are you ready?"

"I'm so ready!"

Pushing into Vedie is better than I ever could have imagined. I feel powerful and at the same time tender as I enter the warmest, tightest, safest place in the world.

I have to pant because it's the only thing I can think to do that will prevent me from coming right here and now, when I'm not even fully inside him—this is how amazing he feels. And once I'm all the way in, I wish time would stand still so I could brand this moment on my memory.

I'm united with Vedie in a way so intimate it almost hurts. I search the expression on his face to assure it's equally magical for him.

"Please, Teo, move...please move inside me..." And since I could never say no to such a plea, I begin to gently thrust.

As soon as I establish my rhythm, I drop a hand to his dick. And the first time he groans in pleasure, I'm compelled to speak. "I never knew it could be like this." *Which is because Daniel never made love to me—he raped me.* I don't chase this thought from my mind because it signifies that times in my life have changed so drastically for the better.

I wish I could kiss him as we make love, but I've worked out a position that allows me to close in on my orgasm—and from the sound of his low moans, I believe he's doing the same. My mouth can't reach his lips, so I vow to kiss him the instant we've both let go. The vital moment arrives sooner than I want, but I hold back long enough to feel his wetness as it spills over my fingers, and only then do I fill the condom.

As soon as our tremors stop, I dive down and cover his lips with mine, and resist the inexplicable urge to tell him I love him.

MATT'S JOURNAL DATED AUGUST 2010

Sounds and smells still bring me right back. It amazes me that these senses are in some ways more powerful than sight.

*The sound of oil sizzling in a pan tells me duct tape is about to be ripped off my face and my wrists and my ankles.

*The smell of bacon frying is a reminder I'd better grease up my ass fast if I don't want to get ripped apart.

*The sound of a satisfied belch indicates it's time for me to "get into position" as Daniel used to say. In other words, lie belly-down on the bed.

*When the smell of perspiration is heavy in the air, I automatically tense my thighs, readying myself to be painfully split in two.

Each and every time I encounter these smells and sounds, I'm genuinely shocked when the torture doesn't begin.

Chapter Nine

VEDIE

I wake up in the morning alone on Mateo's bed. I'm not going to lie; I halfway expected this. So I search the floor for my pink nighty, and when I find it, pull it over my head. I'm not about to face the music naked, that's for sure. Not so sure I want to face it in a pink nighty.

Mateo's not in the living room or the kitchen. I find him pumping iron out on the porch. He doesn't seem to notice me standing in the doorway until I clear my throat real loud, and he glances over.

"Morning, Vedie." He smiles, but it's not warm. "I hope you slept well."

"Slept good but woke up alone."

He bends and drops the weight he's holding so it bounces on the padded wooden floor. "Sorry. I'm not much for sleeping in."

"It's barely eight. That's not exactly what I'd call sleeping in."

The man doesn't bend to pick up another dumbbell. Instead, he tilts his head and asks, "Are you okay this morning?"

No, Mateo, I'm not okay at all. I'm scared of getting the big heave-ho because you can't handle being involved with somebody like me. I'm scared of Joey's revenge. I'm scared shitless that Tyrone and Marcus and Juan are going to find out where I'm hiding and come down here to "knock the bitch outta me."

"Of course I'm okay. Except I'm starving." Sometimes I lie.

"Then let's eat."

He walks past me into the kitchen, turning sideways in the doorway so he doesn't have to rub up against my chest. I'm not feeling soft and sweet and girlish any more, so I head off to the bathroom where my duffel bag is stuck in the corner to change into a T-shirt and shorts and my dude attitude.

Five boxes of cereal are on the table when I come into the kitchen. Kids' cereals—the sugary kinds Mama wouldn't get us because she said they'd rot our teeth, and she couldn't afford a dentist bill—and a big gallon jug of milk.

"All we need are spoons and bowls. And the sugar bowl." Mateo grabs two bowls from the cabinet above the sink and pulls out a drawer to get some utensils.

"Are you fuckin' with me? More sugar?" I fill my bowl with something chocolaty that's got little colorful bits of candy in it. "This stuff is made of sugar, dude."

"Never can have too much sweet."

"Your mama doesn't seem to be the type of lady to fill her kid with sugar-candy cereal." Nope. Mrs. North has Fiber One written all over her.

His eyes turn dark. "I spent a lot of time in another place when I was young, and I lived on this stuff." He pours a bowl of something cinnamon-sweet and then sprinkles a shit ton of sugar on top. "Guess I became addicted to starting my day with a sugar high."

"That's a fact." I wrinkle my nose but pour on the milk and dive into my cereal. Mateo eats his with a spoon, but dry. Guess he doesn't want to dilute the sugar with milk. "So, what's up with your folks, man? Zero warm fuzzies got passed back and forth between you and them, if you don't mind me saying."

This time, he blinks halfway and his pretty eyes roll back, and for a second, it's as if they've disappeared. When his eyeballs roll down again, he says, "Let's leave that subject alone, Vedie."

Sure, he talks all polite, but he slammed yet another door in my face this morning. Looks like all we're going to share is take-out food and sex that doesn't mean anything. "Uh, sure thing."

"I have to work today. Think you can find something to keep you occupied around here until I take you to the bar?" he asks between shoveled bites of dry cereal. His eyes are glued to the cartoons on the back of the cereal box.

"Yeah. Not a problem." Last night, we got close to each other, but it's ancient history in the light of day. "Maybe instead, you could take me to Sheila's place this morning. Me and her hang out a lot. And she can bring me over to the bar this afternoon seeing as she's on the clock tonight too."

"Sounds good." He doesn't look my way, and I wonder what the hell I'm doing here with a dude who's more fucked-up than me.

SHEILA AND ME got to be fast friends right off the bat at The Only Tiki Hut. The first time we met at work, we bumped into each other—I mean literally—when her hip had smashed into my ass over by the bar. She sassed me and I sassed her right back—and that was it. After laughing our butts off, we swapped phone numbers.

I usually love going to Sheila's apartment. When I visit, she makes it "all about Vedie," and who doesn't get into that shit? Nobody's ever done anything for me before, and I got misty the first time or two she pampered me, but now I'm almost used to it. Today, though, I'm over here in a dude mood, which doesn't happen too much.

"Are you hungry, Vedie?" We're sitting in her sunny yellow kitchen; it's all clean and sparkly and homey.

"Nah, ain't hungry. I'm all filled up on chocolate cereal."

Sheila wrinkles her nose because she's a health food addict. "How about a cup of tea then?"

I nod and at the same time fight the tears that want to spill down my face. Not because she's treating me so nice, this time, but just because I'm all worked up.

Sheila's got a roommate who's cool too. Right now, Betsy's sitting across the table from me, painting her fingernails this kickass blackish-purple color that matches her hair. "Vedie, are you sure you don't want me to do your nails? I can file them square, oval, or squoval, and give you a hand massage, too." Betsy's in beauty school in Windward, so she's always trying out new skills on me. She did a freaking awesome job on my eyebrows last week. She fans her hand in front of me. "You likey?"

Squoval fingernails rock, but it's not the right time for a manicure. "I like it fine...but I'm not in the mood." Betsy and Sheila know what it means when I tell them I'm not in the mood: I'm not feeling my feminine side.

Sheila drags her chair out of the ray of sunshine beaming through the window and sits at the end of the kitchen table where it's shady. She pushes my mug of tea across the table to me. "Here, drink your tea. You'll feel better."

I blow on the hot liquid to cool it down and take a small sip. "OMG—pear flavor!"

"Nothing but the best for you, hun." Sheila takes a sip of her tea and looks at me, real curious. "So what's up with you and Crazy Matt?"

"Good question, girlfriend." I sure wish I knew the answer.

"You guys doing the dirty?" Betsy asks. She's never very subtle.

"What do you take me for? I'm not one to kiss and tell. *Jeez.*"

"Well, this is a change—usually you share so many details about your sexcapades that Sheila and me are screaming, 'TMI, Vedie!'" Betsy's so surprised I'm not blabbing she nearly falls off her chair.

"Hush, Betsy." Sheila's looking at me funny, as if she's trying to figure out Algebra. "You like Matt a lot, don't you?"

"He's not bad." I'm sure my eyes tell the whole story. Everybody always says they do. "We got...you know...super close...last night. In here." I put my hand on my T-shirt over the place where my heart's pounding. Cheesy as shit, but nobody in this kitchen's about to sue me for it. "And then this morning, the dude's cold as a Frozen Caramel Coolatta. Got brain freeze when I tried to tell him good morning."

"You don't need that shit, Vedie." Betsy doesn't take crap from anybody. "Dump his ass."

Sheila's more understanding. "Betz, Matt isn't your everyday ordinary gorgeous hunky asshole. He's...he's sort of damaged."

Damaged. It's a good word for Mateo, so I say, "Something's definitely messed up his mind. I think probably it went down back when he was a kid." An image of little Rosita flashes in my brain—her skinny body lying on the sidewalk, the light snuffed out of her eyes.

"You don't have to let the fact that this guy's Mr. Screwed-Up-America mess with your mind, you know. You don't owe it to him to fix his broken ass." Betsy stands and starts waving her hands around, trying to dry her fingernails fast.

"I don't think Mateo wants me to fix him." My special pear tea doesn't taste so sweet anymore. "But still, he needs somebody. He's too scared to need, though. So he runs." And just like that, a light bulb clicks on in my brain, and I can relate. Because I ran too.

Sheila nods with understanding. Betsy rolls her eyes and waves her hands around even faster.

"I was alone up north in Boston. I needed somebody to be my person. You know, the one I could turn to. But there wasn't anybody."

"What has that got to do with Matt being an asshole and shutting you out this morning, after he got what he wanted from you last night?" Betsy sits back down and reaches for Sheila's tea. These two share everything it seems. "Gimme a goddamned break!"

I'm not stupid; I get what Betsy's saying. It would likely serve me well to pay attention, but I'm still kind of pissed off.

"He might hurt you." Sheila's eyes are wide. The tone in her voice is a warning.

"Been hurt before."

Betsy shakes her head, leans back, and sucks down the rest of Sheila's tea.

I say a prayer to anybody up there who's listening. The prayer's about accepting a person the way he is, because that's what Matt's done for me, and it's what I should do for him too. Even if it might come back and bite me in the ass, I plan to take him as he is.

And the tea tastes sweet again. It does.

MATT'S JOURNAL DATED JANUARY 2011

When I was about ten, I tried to establish a human connection with Daniel. It was an effort in futility. Hindsight makes this clear, I guess. Looks as if this damned journal is serving its purpose.

I looked into his eyes on many occasions, desperately needing to see something human there. For so long, Daniel was the only one I had. He was my only choice, my only chance. And because of this, I badly needed to know he had the capacity to feel. And that he had feelings for me. Love, compassion, pity... I'd take anything.

But every time I dared to look, the only thing I saw in his eyes were two deep black holes fixed on me with lust and hostility. What alternative was there for me but to consider this a valid form of human interaction?

Lust and hostility: the basis of my single social bond from the age of seven until fifteen. Sadly, it was as clear to me then as it is now that Daniel's humanity—at least in terms of compassion and love—was in the "off" position. And so I switched "off" as well. Lust and hostility had to be enough for me, and so they were.

Like "father," like "son."

MATT

After I drop Vedie off at Sheila's apartment, I drive around for a long time. I'm not ready to return to the cottage. I'm not ready to focus on my computer and my business. I'm definitely not ready to see Vedie, which is beside the point because he's at Sheila's place.

It hits me that my home has been invaded by a stranger, and all I want is to climb into a deep hole and pull the dirt down on top of my head. I want to go back to the safety of my waterfront cottage "hiding spot," but I'm sharing it, temporarily at least, with Vedie. And I offered to do this. In fact, I *insisted* he invade my solitary escape.

I should have known better.

By the time I was in middle school, I'd learned to embrace the status quo, and I've been doing it ever since. Life as I know it, even if it's hell, is a safe hell. But the unknown...is absolutely terrifying.

And right now I'm terrified.

It's tough to be broken and unfixable and at the same time still wanting more out of life.

I turn the truck around and head back to the cottage to face my cats and my business and Vedie's duffel bag filled with enough men's and women's attire to last him for weeks...and to face my life.

Chapter Ten

VEDIE

Staying with Mateo is safe and not safe at the same time. My body is safe—Joey can't beat on me here, and I eat better than I did when I lived in my little room above the Laundromat. But my heart—I'm not sure exactly how safe my heart is here. But I don't have time to worry about the safety of my heart right now, because I've got to show him how thankful I am he saved my ass.

"Thanks for bringing me by my place so I could grab more of my shit." I'm damned proud of what I've done here. It's the least I could do for this dude who's done so much for me.

Mateo comes into the living room from the kitchen to stand beside me in front of the big bay window. He gawks in an upward direction but says nothing.

"I've got another sheet left over so I can make a swag curtain for the bedroom, too." I tuck in the edge of the curtains I made from my pink rainbow-patched sheets that now drape over the living room window like a little window toga. "What do ya think? You cool with them?"

I'm scared to take a look at Mateo's face, because the man's eyes tell so many of his thoughts, same as mine. He won't be able to hide it if he freaking hates what he sees. When I finally check him out, his eyes are squinting, as if he's not too sure what to make of his plain tan-and-brown-and-gray living room getting happy pink curtains.

"I…I…" It's all he says before he rubs his eyes.

"I can pull them off in less time than it'd take you to say 'ugly-ass curtains' if the look of them makes you want to hurl." I step right up to the window and reach for the top of the curtain because decorating this window was a dumbass idea, and I should've known better. Mama always used to say I'd always butt in where I didn't belong. Mateo doesn't need any of my *Queer Eye for the Straight Guy* advice in making his living room sparkle.

His fingertips brush my shoulder. "No. Don't take them down, Vedie."

I drop my arms to my sides and turn to face him since I haven't got a clue what's up.

"You don't have to leave ugly-ass curtains on your windows to make me happy, Mateo." I study his face, looking for signs of his true feelings, but he's blank. "It's your house, dude."

His empty gaze traces the top of the window and finally comes back to me. "Don't take them down, Vedie. They look pretty."

I put my hands on my hips and challenge him. "What do you like about them, huh? Tell me!"

Again, Mateo studies the pink curtains, and I figure he's scraping the back of his brain for something nice to say about what I made before he demands I rip them down. "They're fun and happy and…and they remind me of you." His cheeks turn red, and I'd bet my ass that mine do too. "I like them."

Well, shit… Neither one of us can believe what just spilled out of his mouth, so I smooth down my skirt and say, "Then I'm gonna go do the same deal to the bedroom window, okay?"

I don't wait for him to answer, because I need to be alone ASAP so I can play the sweet words he said over and over in my brain.

MATT

It's as if we're playing house. Not that we're in the house right now. We're in the meat department of the Placida Island Stop, Shop, and Save planning this coming week's menu. Because Vedie and I seem to be living together now. Which was my bright idea.

In the grocery store, Vedie is in his element. "I can make us a kick-ass chicken tortilla soup if we get boneless chicken breasts. Do you have fire-roasted tomatoes and a can of black beans in your cupboard?"

I shake my head slowly, hoping the shock that I'm at the grocery store, fully immersed in domestic chatter, doesn't show on my face.

"Then we're gonna need to head down aisle three." Vedie bumps me gently with his hip, and I step aside. The grocery cart is now in his possession. For a few seconds, I watch him as he struts off toward the poultry case. A resolute smile barges its way up from my gut to my throat to my lips. And once again, I marvel at what I suspect I'm feeling. *Can this be happiness?*

"Veeeedie! Hey, girlfriend! You haven't stopped by in days! Sheila's been worrying her ass off about you. Where've you been?" An athletically built purple-haired lady dressed in a dark camouflage jumpsuit pulls Vedie into her arms and squeezes, then pushes him back to get a look at his face.

"I've been around, but come to think of it, Sheila hasn't been at work for a couple of days," he replies.

"My girl pulled a muscle in her shoulder and had to take time off."

"Shit!" He lifts both hands to cover his mouth, and I know he's upset. I can easily read his body language, and I'm not sure how I feel about this. "You should've told me. I could've helped you guys out."

I learned how to read body language when I was living with Daniel. And I learned this lesson quickly, as it meant the difference between getting swatted twice on the ass with a rolled- up newspaper or taking a full beating to my back with the buckled end of his leather belt.

"*Jeez*. I've got a cell phone, Betsy. One of you two coulda called me." He glances over at me, and I wonder if my lips have started moving as I remember days I'd rather forget.

The purple-haired woman named Betsy hugs him again, with one tattooed arm this time. "I took a few days off from school, so Sheila and me got some quality time together." She waggles her eyebrows, and I assume this "Betsy" person is Sheila's partner. I've known Sheila for at least five years from her job at the tiki bar, and I had no idea she was in a relationship.

"Mateo...come here!" Vedie waves me over to where they're standing by the refried beans. "Mateo, this is my friend, Betsy. She's Sheila's girlfriend."

Obediently, I step to Vedie's side but am suddenly on guard. I don't even have to think about making strides to protect myself from bonding with other human beings; I have an isolationist instinct. My gut involuntarily tightens, and my shoulders stiffen, and I find myself sizing up this stranger in front of me. "Hey." It's all I am willing to say.

"Hey, man. You've been cool to Vedie by letting him bunk with you since that dickhead Joey has been after him."

She reaches out to shake my hand, so I go with it, but I don't give anything away with my body language—not a smile or a hand squeeze. Not a thing. "Yeah."

"Well, my girl Sheila and me owe you one. Vedie's a sweetheart, and he deserves only the good stuff in life." She smiles at Vedie and then at me. "Wanna come over to our place for a few drinks and a movie some night soon? You know...it'd be just the four of us."

Do I look like a guy who gets into a romantic couples' movie night?

I stare at her in disbelief, while still trying to read her intentions.

She stares back, dark eyes confused by my silence, but right before she asks me what my fucking problem is, Vedie swoops in and saves the day.

"I'll give you a call once we check my work schedule, right, Mateo?"

I dip my chin once. Just once.

"Great...then I guess I'll see you around." Apparently unsure of what to make of my stony silence, Betsy sends me a strange look, turns, and walks toward the dairy section.

"You aren't exactly a people person, huh?" Vedie looks at me, blinks once, and then again positions himself behind the grocery cart. "We're gonna need a shit ton of tortilla chips." And he's off.

VEDIE

"How's about you ask me a question, then I ask you one? You know, we take turns...the way kids do." Mateo wants to know more shit about where I come from and how I got to this bum-crack island. And I'm not above using his curiosity to get the info I need about him, which might be called blackmail, but I don't give a crap. Plus, we're into our third bottle of wine, and way beyond tipsy, which I hope is going to loosen his lips even more.

He blinks his golden eyes...once, twice...three times. In between the second and third blinks, his eyeballs roll up into his head, but when they come down again, he's back. Still, he says nothing.

"I'll start. Where'd you grow up?" I lean back on the couch, glass of wine in hand, and bat my lashes a couple times. That should do the trick.

Mateo smirks because it's a tit-easy question and he's not scared of answering it. "My family is from Marblehead, Massachusetts."

I somehow know he lived in a fancy-ass mansion overlooking the ocean. And since he's done good by answering without squirming, I give him a freebie. "Cool. I grew up in a neighborhood called Mattapan. You know, in the city of Boston. So me and you weren't too far away from each other growing up, huh?" Not too far in miles, at least. I've got a feeling in most other ways we were worlds apart.

Again, he allows that devil's smirk. Call me a mind reader, because I know Mateo thinks I'm not aware I just gave up the answer to what was going to be his first question, but I know what I'm doing. Instead of gloating because he pulled one over on me, he looks at me real strange—bug-eyed and tight-lipped—and adds, "I didn't live there, with my family, though. I mean, not for the whole time I was growing up." Slow blinks and a short fadeaway follow, so I don't push him to explain right yet.

"Okay. Your turn, Teo. Ask away."

He's not done staring at me, but he shifts his attention to the bottle of red wine on the coffee table, refills his glass, and glances my way to see if I want more. I shake my head, so he puts the bottle back down and lifts up his glass. "I want to know about your family. Tell me who you lived with and about your neighborhood and—"

"Me and Mama and my two brothers, Tyson and Marcus—and a lot of the time my second cousin Shondra, seeing as her mama wasn't fit to care for her—we all lived on the third floor of this old house. The whole street was big old homes made into apartments, so the area was crowded with people, and everybody knew everybody else's business because you could hear right through the walls. And, let's see…there was a bodega on the corner…and down the street, we had Ryan Park. Typical city living, you know?"

"When did you know…you were different?" He sneaks in another question, and I act like I don't notice he took my turn. "What I mean is…" Mateo gulps down half his glass of wine; he thinks the booze will give him the right words.

"You wanna know when it hit me that I didn't feel all the way a dude in my heart?"

He nods and licks his wine-red lips.

"I knew I wasn't exactly the same as my brothers for forever. Or, at least, for as far back as I can remember. But I wasn't so much confused about it, because it was normal for me." Spelling out this shit isn't as easy as I thought. "See, I wanted to be girlish every now and again, but then being *only* boyish got forced on me." My turn to suck down a gulp or three of liquid courage.

"How did they do it—you know, force you to act the way they thought boys should act?"

But I'm not *that* easy. "Uh, uh, uh." I waggle my finger under his nose. "My turn to ask a question, big dawg." He nods, and I decide on my question. "Where'd you grow up, if it wasn't at home with your family?"

"Um...pass."

"You can't pass on a question, dude."

"I just did." His expression is blank and he closes his eyes. I decide not to push the issue. Not yet.

"Okay, we'll come back to that one." I scramble for another question—I've got so many it's tough to choose. "When did you get this?" I place my finger on the lizard tattoo wrapped around his right forearm. It's not bright and colorful, just a thin black outline. "And why a lizard?"

"It's a chameleon." He says it like I should already know. "Chameleons can hide in plain sight." He turns his body so he's facing away from me and sinks down into the brown couch.

"You mean it can camouflage itself?" I watched lots of nature television shows after I quit high school, so I know major shit about lizards.

"Yes."

"Why a chameleon?" I'm pretty sure I already know the answer, but I still ask.

"I'll pass on that one, too...but I got the tattoo when I was fourteen. Lied and said I was eighteen and got away with it because I was tall for my age."

"Fair enough. But listen, if you pass, you've got to down what's in your glass."

"Fair enough..." He leans back and inhales the rest of his wine. "My turn."

"Yes, sir." I try a little eyelash batting, but he's not looking at me anymore.

"Who tried to force you to act like a boy?" His attention returns to the half-empty bottle on the table. He stares at it as if he can make it pour wine by using mind power, like a Jedi. But finally, he leans forward to do the job with his hands.

I answer as he refills. "Almost everybody. Mama didn't approve when I did stuff folks think only girls should do, like play with dolls and dress up like a princess. She more or less gave my brothers the go-ahead to do whatever they needed to change me."

"Is that how you got those marks on the backs of your thighs?"

"Uh-huh. They used to always whoop me there because they figured it'd sting worse on my skinny legs than on my round butt."

Mateo's lips straighten into a pencil-thin line. "What else did they do to you?"

"You name it; they done it. Beat on me with fists, kicked me with their boots on, whooped me and choked me with a belt. Stuffed me in a closet and left me there—no food or water or nothing until I swore I'd only talk sports and act like a bro." I only listed the kinds of attacks that stick out in my mind as the worst. I'd be here all day if I had to tell Mateo every way they tried to change me.

"In a closet..." He blinks real slow.

And I know he's about to leave—his screwed-up soul is gonna slip out of his perfect body and find a place to rest easy.

But he sticks around to ask one more question. "Did it work?"

Here I sit, wearing black velvet shorts and a silky purple cami, my hair pulled up into what could be called a man bun if I was in a manly mood. "Does it look like it worked?" I point to my outfit.

He lets out a spurt of laughter, and his head is back in the game. "Not so much."

"But I promised I'd try to act only like a boy, after a day in the closet—I wanted a glass of water so bad. So I started faking it as much as I could. The thing is, there's some stuff a person can't bullshit."

"I see." He takes my glass and fills it. "Your turn."

I'm pretty sure he's got a clue where I'm planning to go with my next question because he looks nervous as a cat in a shower stall. "Let's see…you're from Marblehead, but you didn't grow up there…and you won't tell me why. You got a tattoo of a chameleon that hides in plain sight twisted all over your arm, and scars all over your back. You black out when shit gets too heavy. You're not close to anybody, but you always gotta defend me when I'm attacked, like you're super pissed off when folks mess with me."

A full picture of the heart and soul of the man sitting beside me on the couch comes together in my brain. Maybe I'm no book scholar, but I'm no dumbass, either.

He turns to face me. His eyes look lighter and wider and more open than I've ever seen them. I wonder if he *wants* me to know his secret.

"You got abused."

His jaw drops and his eyes get glassy.

"Somebody took you."

His eyes roll back…and he's gone.

MATT'S JOURNAL DATED JUNE 2011

In the emotional "off" position, I slept as much as I could. For some reason, I had little energy, and I no longer conjured up clever ways to escape. I accepted my life because the only alternative I could see was more suffering at Daniel's hands.

Even when I was eventually granted the freedom to roam the streets at about ten years old, I remained separate. I somehow knew I was unlike all the other kids I met on the bike trails near the middle school to smoke cigarettes and drink soda with, or beer, if we could get our hands on it. I was disgustingly different.

Fear was ingrained in me. It had become the biggest part of me, and to this day, it still is. Because of this fear, it never occurred to me I could run away. My existence was all about survival, and Daniel was the only lifeline I could see. If I kept him happy—if I said what he wanted to hear, if I did what he wanted me to do—he'd probably let me live. My fear kept this imbalance of power in the forefront of my mind.

Daniel had all of me from the day I swore I'd do and be whatever he wanted if he'd please stop whipping my back with his belt.

Chapter Eleven

MATT

Once again, I've been drawn to The Only Tiki Hut on Placida Island, as a moth is drawn to the flame. I drink my beer slowly, another brew of Vedie's choice, and I can't help running a long list of discontents through my mind.

I don't like how Joey looks at Vedie's ass when he bends over a table to fill the gray tub with dirty dishes. He's doing it right now, as I swallow my last sip. And seeing this makes my fingers itch with an almost unavoidable need to grasp the older man by the neck of his faded green T-shirt and throttle him until he'll never again be physically able to stand behind Vedie and drool over his body. I close my eyes and mentally go there, just long enough to imagine the pleasure that would be mine if I were to give in to my rage.

"Hey, Matt. Tonight's special is lobster mac and cheese. I tried it—the stuff is legendary." Sheila's smiling at me, and it's a brighter smile than usual, as if she thinks we'll soon be going on a double date together. I don't think I'm comfortable with this.

"Sounds good. I'll take two to go." I want to look away from her smile, but I can't.

"One's for Vedie, right?" Her smile turns into a grin.

My blush gives me away, I'm sure. "And put lots of rolls in the bag, please, and a garden salad, too...heavy on cucumbers."

Another thing I dislike is how I'm starting to know Vedie's preferences. He'll slather the rolls with butter and pick the cucumber slices out of his salad with two fingers and dip them into the ranch dressing he will have poured onto a saucer and close his eyes while savoring his feast.

I don't like that I admitted to Vedie my cat Jennifer is named after Jennifer Aniston, and Bob is actually Sponge Bob Square Pants.

I don't like how when I come back to reality on my living room couch or in my bed—after my mind has shut down because I couldn't handle a question or a smell or a sound—that Vedie is holding me, his arm tight around my shoulders. And how I feel safe—so safe I sometimes pretend I'm not back yet, closing my eyes and letting time stand still while I relish the comfort.

But more than anything else, I don't like that Vedie knows my secret. That I provided him with enough clues to guess it, and I did this intentionally. I wanted him to know because I needed to share in his strength.

I don't like it at all.

And it's why I have to push him away.

Just as I did this morning when I woke up on the couch beside Vedie, practically on top of him, clutching him with greedy fingers as if he's my long-lost security blanket. And to make it worse, he was already awake, looking at me—not with disgust or bewilderment or pity—but with compassion. Maybe even understanding, in a "been there, done that" way. He's known the same kind of fear that is so integral to who I've become.

"I'm done for the night, Teo!" Coming from behind me, Vedie's voice is so bright and cheerful. My response is to simultaneously brace myself for the thrill of his impending nearness and melt from the blend of sweetness and strength I'm becoming addicted to.

"You want to go change your clothes?" I ask. "Our dinner's on its way. Should only be a couple more minutes."

I don't like that I know Vedie well enough to recognize it's the time of night for him to decide if his feminine or masculine side will take it from here.

"Yeah. I'm gonna go grab my backpack and put on a miniskirt!"

VEDIE

"You don't wanna do this, dawg..." I don't need Joey slobbering all over me right now.

"Oh, so you think you know what I want? And you think I want to get with you, huh?"

Truth is, I haven't got a clue what Joey wants tonight. He's not all sexy-acting like he usually is when he gets me alone. He's plain old pissed off, and I'm plain old scared.

"I'm not saying that." I'm glad Angie made this bathroom a free-to-be-whatever-gender-you-wanna-be bathroom, but I sure wish it wasn't way the hell out here in left field, over by the beach volleyball courts.

"Think you're a hottie, or something?"

My brothers used to look at me like I was a piece of trash, but they never looked at me with the pure hate Joey's got in his eyes.

"I wouldn't fuck you if my life depended it, Wilson! Your kind's got diseases I don't need to catch. You fooled me into thinking you was a girl, and dat's the only reason I—"

"Look, I'm gonna head back to the bar and forget this shit ever went down here tonight, man." Easy to say, but I've got a strong feeling I'm not going anywhere.

"You'll limp back to the bar when and if I say you can." Joey's not too tall, but he's got fifty pounds on me, all in his chest and shoulders and belly. He grabs my arm so tight I drop my backpack on the sandy path. "You're coming with me, bitch." His fist is in my hair.

"Joey...man, listen. Mateo's waiting on me at the bar...so you've gotta let me go..." I've been here before—having somebody drag me off by my hair to beat the living crap out of me. So I let out a scream in the hopes it'll catch somebody's attention.

It doesn't take long until Joey's fists have me seeing stars.

MATT

"Your food's got to be ice-cold by now." Sheila says aloud half of what I'm thinking. The other half is: *where the fuck is Vedie?*

I remind myself Vedie's not obligated to come home with me tonight. He probably got a better offer for this evening's lodging. It's not like we're boyfriends; it's possible he doesn't even consider us close friends. All we are is a couple of relative strangers shacking up together temporarily, strictly in the interest of Vedie's safety.

I can tell myself this shit until I'm blue in the face; it won't make it true.

"Vedie's changing in the bathroom," I reply blandly.

"Well, I guess perfectly applied makeup *does* take time." Sheila winks at me again, and I get that funky "we're BFF's" vibe.

A few more minutes pass, and I can't sit still any longer. I'm not the kind of guy to wait for my date outside the bathroom door, my foot tapping impatiently, but this could be because I'm also not a guy who has ever had a date to wait for. I sigh loudly and admit that things have changed. Although I'm not sure I'm comfortable with this, I head out in search of Vedie, past the bar and across the volleyball courts to the path that leads to the gender-neutral restroom.

Something on the edge of the path catches hold of my ankle, and I stumble. I reach down and unhook a leopard-print backpack from my foot. "What the fuck?"

But I already know the answer. This is Vedie's backpack. For some reason, I turn it over and examine the zipper, and actually go so far as to pull the zipper over the top so the bag gapes open. Inside, I see his neatly folded green T-shirt and khaki shorts. His sneakers are underneath, his socks rolled into little balls and tucked inside. For some reason, the sight of those socks makes me wince. I imagine his feet, so brown and graceful, tucked delicately beneath him on my couch.

"Vedie!" My feet are frozen on the sand. And I'm the ice sculpture standing in them, stiff and unmoving.

Someone took him...grabbed him. Vedie's gone...

Oh, Jesus!

"Vedie!" My cry is ragged and desperate.

Oh, Vedie...where are you...don't be lost from me...don't be gone...

With his backpack slung over my shoulder, I get my ass in gear. I bolt to the bathroom to see if he's in there, trying to tame his unruly hair or applying some of the sweet, shiny gloss to his lips, but when I push the door open, the room is empty.

"Vedie! Can you hear me?" I shout irrationally into the small room.

I stop and listen for a reply I'm certain isn't going to come, and then I'm off, searching the shrubbery along the sides of the path. There's a single overhead light above the entrance to the bathroom brightening the area, but it doesn't do much in terms of visibility off the path. So I grab my cell phone out of my pocket and turn on the flashlight, scramble around in the grass and low bushes, tripping often and falling to my knees every now and then, frantic with the sure knowledge that Vedie will suffer my seven-year-old fate should I not succeed in this desperate search.

I stumble my way to the beach where the flames on the tiki torches have been doused and it's completely dark, aside from the few remaining lights reflecting off the distant bar. I have no plan in mind, no clever scheme as to how I'm going to find him. I rush back and forth on the sand without rhyme or reason, the small stream of light from my cell phone barely illuminating the way.

And then I hear it.

A moan, deep and throaty. Human. I head toward it, which happens to be down by the water.

"Is that you, Vedie?" No answer. Not even another dull groan to lead me to him.

After forcing myself to stand still and listen for a full minute, I finally hear another sound, like a gift from some distant God who never before has acknowledged my prayers. This time, the moan is a word.

"Nooooo…"

"I'm coming!" I move toward the haunted sound, and within a few seconds, I'm standing in the surf. *This can't be good*, I think, but I continue to search until I come upon a wet lump of human being, half-submerged in water.

Thank God his head is on the sand and not in the water.

I honestly don't think I can handle this.

Is all this wetness on his head salt water...or is some of it something else...something more vital to his life?

I scoop Vedie into my arms, carry him to dry sand, and set him down gently. Then I shine the light from my phone onto his face and gasp with relief when I see no blood. But from firsthand experience, I know better than to think he's unharmed—there are many ways to hurt someone that don't require bloodshed.

His eyes flutter open. "I'm...I'm leaving this island." He turns his head to the side and vomits mostly water. "There's no place safe for a person like me."

I know what shock is. I've seen Vedie in shock before. *I've* been in shock before...

His eyes are empty and he's trembling.

"Who did this to you?" At the moment, this isn't the most important consideration, but I can't hold back the question. I have a strong suspicion as to the culprit, but without confirmation, I can't be sure whose ass I'm going to beat.

I shine the light on the ground as Vedie struggles to his feet. His pretty, jeweled flip-flops are missing, and the buttons have been ripped from his favorite white blouse. He drags his fingers down the column of his throat, from chin to collarbone, and coughs softly. "Everybody does this to me."

Suddenly coming alive, he snatches the backpack from my hand and tosses it to his feet. Right there on the beach, I watch as he transforms. He rips the wet blouse from his shoulders and lets it fall to the sand. He drags his short denim skirt and light-colored panties over his hips, down his legs, and kicks them away with so much force I can't see where they land in the distant darkness.

The person standing in front of me, completely naked in the night, is truly straddling genders. A blank space of a being—his hands rise again, and this time, fingers rake through wild, damp curls blowing in the ocean breeze.

I feel an intense connection with this person, as I see a reflection of myself in him. Because just as Vedie's soul is caught somewhere between genders, I'm trapped between man and boy. And in these ways, society sees us as flawed.

Time stands still as we assess ourselves, and each other, on the beach. I have no idea how long we stand there; it could as easily have been a minute as an hour. One by one, most of the lights at the bar go out, and finally, in the near pitch-black darkness, Vedie's shaking stops. My eyes, now accustomed to the night, can make out his form bending gracefully and lifting the pack, pulling out the T-shirt and shorts, and emerging in his most masculine form.

"Let's go," he says, slinging the backpack over his shoulder, and he staggers up the beach toward the restaurant. I trail behind in the direction of the one remaining light—weak, bluish, and flickering in the distance.

VEDIE IS BY nature a talker, but tonight he's silent. I don't like it—not being one to embrace even small changes in my routine—and I want the silence to end. It's up to me to figure out how to fix this—to fix him—but I suspect it's impossible. I have no idea what to do to help him. All I know is tonight he's broken in a way I haven't seen before.

Why do I care so much?

I'm angry that I care at all.

He's curled up on the bed, again naked, and I sense he's still caught between genders, not feeling soft and sweet or bold and steady. His clothes seem to be the main way he expresses his gender identity, and tonight's nakedness seems to be a manifestation of his confusion.

"I brought you some water." I set the glass down on the bedside table. "You've been coughing a lot and...I thought it might help."

"Thank you." After icing his face for too short a time, Vedie has pulled the covers up to his nose, and now resembles a root vegetable, his dreads a flurry of leaves poking up from the ground. All I can see is the top of his face, crowned by an unruly mop of hair.

I climb onto the bed next to him, but I don't turn off the light. "You want to...you know...want to talk about what happened tonight?"

He answers without hesitation. "I got beat up."

"Was it Joey? Did Joey do this to you?"

"Does it matter who did it?" He sits and turns to me. For the first time, I see the red mark of fingerprints around his neck—fresh bruises mingling with crescent-shaped fingernail scratches, evidence of his efforts to pull away the squeezing hands. "Anywhere I go...*everywhere* I go...there's gonna be somebody to knock me around because I don't fit into the gender boxes."

The crimson marks on his neck shock me, but his words actually make me gasp. "No...that's just not right."

"Shit that isn't right happens every day, dude. You know this better than anybody." The Vedie I've come to know isn't here tonight, and I wonder if there's yet another personality dwelling inside him I'm only just meeting.

"He choked you?"

"Tried to dunk my head and strangle me, too. At the same time—twice the fun." He tries to smile, but his effort is futile. "The dude has serious anger issues."

"So it *was* Joey?"

"Not gonna say. But I have to leave this island, big dawg." He lies down again, this time flat on his back. After a loud sigh, he speaks, but quieter than before. "It's not safe for me here anymore."

A rug I didn't even know was tucked beneath my feet is ripped away, and I'm thrown off-balance. "No."

Staring at the ceiling, his voice lacks expression. "Face it—you and me are nothing to each other. Not even fuck buddies, because you can depend on your fuck buddy, and I've got no idea what to expect out of you. You saved my ass, and I'm thankful as hell, but starting tomorrow, your duty's done. Because I'm gone." He turns onto his side so he's facing away from me. "Can you hit the light? I'm beat."

I lean over and turn out the light. My brain races; my lips move in the darkness.

I don't want him to go, but I have no right to ask him to stay. I'm too broken a man to offer him anything lasting, even friendship.

I wish I could close my eyes and escape to that place where there's no pain or fear or trace of emotion—I could float to the ceiling and look down at my pathetic self as I suffer with self-induced pain. But disassociation doesn't work that way. I'm not in charge of it; it's in charge of me. I rarely question its hold on me anymore. And tonight, I'm left here on the bed, fully aware of every speck of my pain.

"Can I hold you?" My first impulse is to wonder if I was the person who asked this absurd question. Upon realizing it was indeed me, I struggle not to take it back.

"I'm feeling all the way a man right now." Vedie's voice is flat. "I don't need to get held."

"I don't care if you feel like a man or a woman or something in between. I never have." The silence following my words is long and painful. But I wait because fair is fair. He has suffered through my leaden silences too many times to count.

"Okay. You can hold me, Mateo."

So I do something I've never done before. I turn onto my side, open my arms, and pull another human being right up against my body. And I let my soul seep into his. I do this for my benefit, as well as Vedie's. And I do this because I don't have the right words to express how I feel, but I need to show him I care.

Maybe I even need to own how much *I* care.

If I were a braver man, I would admit I cling to him now because I don't want him to ever leave me. I'm simply not that brave.

VEDIE

My throat feels as if somebody tried to choke the life out of me, which isn't a coincidence; Joey did his damn best to strangle me. I chuckle at my own joke, but it hurts, so I cut it short. I lean up on one elbow and reach across Mateo to grab the glass of water. Swallowing is tough. I get it done, and then I try to stifle a cough. But everybody knows when you try not to cough you just have to cough worse. This is how I end up waking him.

"Sorry, man. Go on back to sleep."

Mateo looks at me with sleepy eyes. I stick the glass back on the table, and when I'm leaning halfway over, he grabs onto me by my arms. "Don't go."

"What?"

"You can't leave. You don't even have bed sheets anymore."

We both glance up at the rainbow-patch sheet I draped over the window.

"That's no reason to stay where I'm gonna get my ass kicked, or worse."

Mateo flips us around so I'm underneath him, and he stares down into my eyes like I matter. "Take a little time off work and hang out here while we sort out what happened last night. It won't put a strain on me...financially, or otherwise. To start with, you can report Joey to the police, and once he's been arrested, then you can go back to work."

"Teo, I never said it was Joey who did this." I touch my throat. "And I've got no choice but to work. Got no cash if I don't hold a job." This situation sucks enough without Mateo pointing out the obvious: no work, no pay. "The fact is, you're not gonna miss me one bit when I'm gone. I'm a sorry pain in your ass who brings down trouble everywhere I go because I'm not normal." I push him off to the side and swing my legs over the edge of the bed, my back to him.

"Stay, Vedie. You can do all the cooking for us...just as if it's your job. I'll pay you for it. And you can do our laundry and some cleaning, too. I seriously need a break from cooking and cleaning because I have a huge work project due from a new account." I'm not sure if he's trying to convince me or himself. "You can't keep running, Vedie."

Mateo has never looked so needy before. If I didn't know better, I'd think he gives a shit about me.

"If I don't work, big dawg, I can't pay the rent on my room in town. And rent is due in a week and a half. I've got to tell my landlord I'm moving out so—"

"You can give notice to your landlord and move your belongings here. All of them. I have plenty of room." He crawls across the bed and sits beside me on the edge. He's still looking at me as if he cares—like he's almost ready to get down on his knees and beg, which doesn't make any sense because I know the man can't care about anybody.

But there's a question I have to ask, and I figure I'll stick around only if he gives me the answer I need. "Why do you really want me to stay?"

I feel his fear. It's a solid thing, a wall that has popped up between us. But somehow, Mateo knocks it down.

"You make breathing worth the effort. So please stay."

Call me a sucker, but his reason works just fine.

Chapter Twelve

MATT'S JOURNAL DATED OCTOBER 2011

Everyone wanted to know. From the journalist who slipped into my backyard where I was supposedly safe from the public's prying eyes, to Mr. Melin, my math teacher at Marblehead High, to my very own mother—it was the most asked and most dreaded question: "Why didn't you run away from Daniel when you had the chance?" Even back then, I picked up on the underlying, not-so-well-hidden suggestion in the question—that it was my fault I was gone so long: "You could have said or done something to get back home. But you didn't."

The thing is, I couldn't answer that question or refute the suggestion. For a long time, years and years, in fact, I thought it was because I didn't know the answer. Time and again random people—my older brother or a kid at school or a police officer—would ask me, "Why didn't you at least *try* to escape? I mean, the guy let you out of the house to ride your bike, and you even had the freedom to go to school. So why didn't you tell somebody your name and that you'd been abducted?" Each time I was posed with this question, all I could do was shrug and walk away.

But journals are meant for soul-searching, and I've been free of Daniel for more than a decade now, so I suppose it's past time I figured this thing out. As in, right now. Today. There's no better time than the present, people say. Not that I care much what anybody says.

So, this time I'm asking myself: Why did I stay with the man who stole me from my family, beat me mercilessly, and raped me every day, when I technically had the freedom to leave?

My silence on the subject suggests I somehow wanted to stay with Daniel. That he'd become exactly what he'd forced me to call him: my dad. But the little boy inside me who never could and still can't find the right words, screams, "No! That's not how it was!"

In hindsight, my thinking may seem faulty, but I was just a kid, and I was reacting to intense fear. Fear of pissing Daniel off in any small way, because it meant being beaten until I couldn't walk, and fear that came from my absolute certainty he'd kill me if he caught me trying to escape. In fact, he told me straight out I wouldn't see another morning if he caught me running. I believed him—who wouldn't?

And so my best bet seemed to be not to make a move. I told myself, in a ten-year-old way, to go with it...be Daniel's son in public and his sex slave behind closed doors.

I played along and shut the fuck up in order to survive.

My plan was about as simple as it sounds: do whatever Daniel tells you to do. It was my key to living one more day, which was my goal, both short and long term.

And now I've solved the daunting personal mystery that has loomed over me for so long. Sure, I feel some relief, I guess. Though it's not as if I'm going to go shouting my big news from the rooftops. I'm sure I'll never have an occasion to share this revelation with another living being, aside from furry purring ones, but at least I think I get where I was coming from, back in the darkest days of my life.

WE'VE CALLED A truce of sorts. Time stands still in a way I like. In a way that takes the pressure off us to make any broad declarations or major decisions or commitments of any kind. But, this isn't true, really, because Vedie did take some time alone on the porch to make a few phone calls I'm sure were difficult for him. It's damned brave of him to trust me enough to take a leave of absence from his job and not renew his monthly lease. Nothing like taking a leap of faith.

Vedie steps into the kitchen and stands in front of the table where I'm trying, without much success, to concentrate on writing a business blog post. "Angie isn't pleased with me. She told me my job probably isn't gonna be waiting when I decide it's time to get off my ass and come back to work." He's noticeably shaken by what he's done. "And my landlord said...he said I've got to get my shit out of the apartment before the end of the month. Dude, you've got yourself a roommate."

I feel about as shell-shocked as Vedie looks. I have a fucking roommate. And even if I'm not exactly sure how this happened, I take full responsibility. I did this to myself.

"I'm thinking I'll get going on the laundry and fix us some supper." He turns toward the cabinets and stands there for a few seconds, a deer in headlights as he waits for me to support his plan.

"You're not my damned slave, Vedie. You can go stretch out on the sand and lounge the afternoon away if you feel like it. I only offered you a way to earn your keep, if you felt you needed one." My message is heartless, and I know I'm withholding the validation he needs.

He nods, not at me, but at the cabinets. "I'm gonna earn my keep, Mateo."

"Fine, if it's what you want. But if you want to be purely my guest, that works for me, too."

"You get your mind on business and leave the rest to me." I almost miss the next thing he says because it comes out as little more than a whisper. "I won't let you down."

Within an hour, spicy soup is bubbling on the stovetop in my largest pot. Vedie is standing beside the kitchen table folding my socks into neat rolls. There's something incredibly warm and homey about this scene that makes my throat tighten and my skin prickle.

"Can't you do your folding someplace else? It's distracting me from my work." My goal isn't to hurt him, but I can't let this living situation make me feel all warm and hopeful...and complacent. I can't allow myself to become accustomed to his sweetness, to his humor, to his very presence. I need to continue to remind us both that what we have here is a "living situation" not a life together.

"Oh...uh...sure. I'll take the laundry into the living room." He picks up the basket but doesn't go anywhere. I know he's looking at me. I can feel the weight of his stare on my face, and it's heavy. I'm sure his aqua eyes are round and confused and wounded.

And he's wondering why I let him into my house, but not my heart.

So I don't look into his eyes. First of all, I don't want our gazes to meet and have him see two black pits of cruel emptiness looking back at him, like the ones I saw when I looked into Daniel's eyes. And I also don't want to see the pain I cause, when at every opportunity, I push him away. Even when I want nothing more than to pull him close.

Instead of fixing his splintered soul, I'm tearing it apart.

VEDIE

I haven't been feeling soft and sweet in days; I wonder if Mateo notices a big part of me is gone. But the way it is around here lately—kind of chilly, real quiet—well, I don't feel comfortable enough to show the other side of me.

This morning, I'm fixing up his living room. I already dusted and vacuumed up the cat hair, and before that, I got a nice dinner casserole started—the one with cream of mushroom soup and chicken and rice Mama used to make—and it's in the oven cooking. Smells like back home, and it makes me all misty. But I'm not going to be a useless burden on Mateo. I refuse to sit around moping, even if he says it'd be okay with him.

I spent the past couple hours cutting all these funky shapes out of my stretchy lace off-the-shoulder top, and now I'm sewing the last one onto a square of fabric I cut from my best purple silky cami using a needle and thread I found in the top bathroom drawer. Yesterday, I saw a beat-up black frame leaning against the corner chair on the screened porch, and Mateo said I could have it. Good thing I've got so many colors of nail polish—made it easy to cover up the cat scratches with tiny flowers.

I stick the fabric design into the frame and close it up. When I flip it over, I smile because I made a fine piece of art that'll make this living room feel like somebody actually lives in it.

Hated like hell to go searching through Mateo's storage closet for a hammer and nail without asking for permission, but I did it because it sucks to bother him while he's working so hard on his computer. I step onto the couch and make a wish he won't fly off the handle at me for banging a hole in his wall—some guys've got a thing about that kind of shit. I only hit the nail three times, and it sits there just perfect to hang the picture I made. Within a couple of seconds, the pretty framed picture of lacy hearts and circles, and shapes that don't have names, all popping out on a purple background, is hanging on the wall above the couch.

Guess the banging noise caught Mateo's attention. I don't even have time to get down off the couch when he steps into the room, and soon, he's gawking at the wall art.

As usual, he doesn't say a word when he sees the picture, and I don't have a clue if he likes it or hates it. But I'm brave, and I step down off the couch to stand beside him.

"You cut up your lacey top."

"And my silky cami too. Look underneath the shapes, and you can see the purple."

"You didn't have to cut your clothes up to—"

"I don't have any other stuff to use to make art with, big dawg." Mateo still hasn't said he thinks it's pretty.

"All you had to do was ask, and I'd have taken you to the craft store." The meaning of his words is sweet honey, but the tone of his voice is a knife that can cut me open, and his face is a stone he can use to crush me into powder. *Not safe.*

I drop my ass onto the couch, sticking my hands into my wild-ass hair because it looks as if I screwed up again. "I'll take it down and stick it in my big duffel bag. If it's not a problem, I can take the thing with me when I move on out of here."

The feeling in the room changes fast. It's like a surge of Mateo's panic pushes the dead calm out of the air. He comes over to the couch and drops onto his knees in front of me. "It's just that...I don't know what to say...that you...did this for me." He's breathing too quick.

"Truth is, I did it for *us*. I get into looking at pretty shit when I'm at home. I just keep on forgetting this ain't my home. It's yours."

A waterfall of changes goes down in his eyes in the next couple of seconds. First off, I swear those pretty eyes get all misty, the way mine always do. Next, they roll up into his skull and stay there for a while. But when they finally roll back, he looks at me again and rubs his eyes with his thumbs. "No."

Seems I've got no clue about life. Every time I do shit I think is going to work out good, it doesn't turn out right. Plus, I don't feel like myself living here. I haven't felt soft and sweet in so long...and I miss that part of me. "I've got to leave here, Teo. It's not working out too good, I don't think."

On his knees beside me, Mateo's frozen like an ice sculpture. "No." This time he says it louder.

"Sheila and Betsy will let me stay with them until I get my act together, so no worries about me being homeless." I lower my hand so my palm lands on the side of his face, and I don't miss how he jerks back, but still, I curve my hand around his cheek. "You've done right by me, Mateo, and I want you to know I thank you for it."

His light-brown eyes lift up until our gazes lock. But his teeth are gritted tight—as if I'm kicking him hard in the belly, except I'm only giving him what he wants most: to be alone again.

"Now, listen, I want you to keep the curtains I made. They make your cottage more...you know...more cheerful. Think of them as my way of saying thanks."

I swear the man is shaking, as if an earthquake is going on inside of his body. And like he's trying his very hardest to not slip into that place he goes when he can't cope. "No."

I ignore this "no," just the way I ignored the other two. "I'll pack up my shit. Won't take me long because a bunch of it's still back at my apartment."

When I try to get up, he grasps my wrists with two needy claws.

"Let me...please, Vedie...I want...just give me another chance to try."

His eyes—they're dry as bone and as cold as ice. But his strange words and his choked-up voice and the terrible trembling—he's feeling shit I don't know a goddamn thing about.

"Try? Try what, Mateo?"

He sighs, and it hurts to hear because it sounds like confusion and fear and pain all rolled up into a breath that has to escape. "Can we try to be..." Another one of those hurtful sighs. "I want us to be more than we've been."

"More...like friends? So you're gonna open up yourself to me?"

"Friends, yeah. It's what I want...so let me try." His eyes, still dry, seem wider. "Please, Vedie. I...I..."

"You what?"

"I've never done it before. The friendship thing...and the opening-up thing. It's all new to me."

"You've never done the I-got-a-life thing, huh?"

He smiles a small scared smile. "I guess not."

"And you think you're not a young dog anymore, so you can't learn a new trick, like how to be a friend."

He nods.

"And you're willing to try, which is real nice. But you've got to know this—I'm not asking you to change. Because keep it in mind, dude, no matter how much you want *me* to change for you, I can't. I can't be different than the way I am."

He doesn't even have to think it over. "I don't want you to change."

I stand, take him by the hand, and help him to his feet.

Together, we look up at the picture I made. "Do you like it?"

Mateo smiles again, bigger this time. "I do. I like it. But I also liked the way the lace top looked on you."

"You did?"

"A lot."

My whole body gets warm, and I know the soft side of me finally wants to come out. I feel safe and wanted. "I'm gonna go to the bathroom for a minute, Teo." I turn and walk away, but my sensitive side is in full bloom before I've left the living room.

MATT

This old dog...well, he has some potential.

We're at Sheila and Betsy's apartment on some sort of a double date, and part of me thinks it's stupid and useless for us to be here—all snuggled together on this puffy, flowery couch watching *Gone Girl*—and that the only thing having friends can do is give me something else to lose. But then I look at Vedie's face, and I forget my worries. His expression is so bright and cheerful, as if simply sitting close beside me eating microwave popcorn out of a bag, with his friends across the room perched on an equally gaudy love seat, makes him feel like a prince...or a princess. It's his choice, really, because I appreciate him both ways.

And I have to stare at him and wonder. Because it's amazing how he's able to push past the hurt and move forward in life. His family drove him off as if he was worthless, and they probably did it violently. Joey attacked him twice, and I haven't exactly been a prize in the friendship or lover department. But here he sits, as if he hasn't got a care in the world, enjoying what he has, instead of fuming over what he's lost.

A flood of feeling for this man washes over me, and I don't know what to do with it. If this had happened yesterday, before I made the decision to change, I would probably have said something cruel and then moved away from his side. But yesterday, I told him I'd change—that I'd start acting like a friend. That I'd be his friend. So, instead of turning away from him, I place my arm on the back of the couch and nod in invitation. After staring at me for a few seconds, probably wondering what the hell I'm doing, he puts the popcorn bag aside and snuggles up against me. I'm so stunned I made a move I almost can't breathe.

I made a move on Vedie, and not a friendship move, either. It was the gesture of a lover. And I'm cool with it.

Betsy and Sheila are more than cool with it—they're staring at us and grinning. And all I want is to float away, but I don't. I fight to stay present. I fight to be here with Vedie.

"You two are so cute!" Sheila is about as satisfied with our cozy situation as Vedie is. I try not to squirm.

But Vedie's conspicuously quiet. He glances down to his hands folded neatly on his lap beside the empty popcorn bag. "We're missing the movie," he says quietly as he fiddles with the flower-shaped button on his denim shorts and stares at the television.

"Hey, look, Sheila, Vedie's acting shy. I think our girly's in love, huh?" Betsy's teasing voice seems to echo in the small room. And although the movie is blaring, it's as if her voice is the only sound.

Vedie's neck and shoulders stiffen. He leaps up, bolts across the room, and soon we hear the front door slam. The three of us stare at each other.

Sheila slaps Betsy's arm. "Nice move, Betz."

"I was only teasing. Shit, Shelia, I always tease him."

Sheila nods in my direction. "Maybe everything's different...with Matt."

Suddenly, they're on the same wavelength, both of them nodding in unison. And it's time for me to make my second big move of the night. So, I stand and say, "Thanks for the good meal, but I think I better go outside and check on Vedie. You know, I should make sure he's not falling apart."

"Vedie's strong. He won't fall apart." Sheila seems sure of this.

I'm less sure. "I'm going to see how he's doing, anyway." I smile as best I can, which probably isn't very good at all, and head for the door.

Betsy and Sheila follow. "Sorry it ended this way tonight, Matt," Betsy offers. "Tell Vedie I know he's not a girl. I was just kidding around."

I open the door. "It'll be our turn to fix a meal for you guys soon." Then I head for the truck, and when I see Vedie in the passenger seat, I breathe a sigh of relief. "Vedie..."

He's got his head in his hands, crying softly, and I immediately remember how vulnerable he becomes when he's upset.

"You want me to take you home so you can take off your makeup and change into sweatpants? I'll find *Gone Girl* on Netflix. We can suck down a few brews and watch the ending."

He looks up at me, his face streaked with green mascara. I reach past him and grab a tissue from the box in my truck. I start to pass it to him but change my mind. With a couple of fingers, I steady his stubbly chin and take it upon myself to wipe his eyes. He lets me clean his face without looking away from me once.

"There you go. No more tears, okay?"

"I'm sorry." He looks away.

"Sorry for what?" Before he can answer, I walk around the truck to the driver's seat and climb in. "You didn't do anything to be sorry for."

"I'm sorry for what Betsy said…about me being…"

There it is. Vedie's embarrassed that Betsy said he's in love with me, and I find myself hoping he's so upset because the truth hurts. "That's nothing to worry about."

We drive home in silence, but my thoughts are racing, and I'm holding on to the here and now with everything I've got.

When we get home, Vedie doesn't change his clothes as I expect him to. He goes to the bathroom, washes his face, and pulls his hair into a knot on the top of his head. But when he comes out, he's wearing the same tiny denim shorts and floral blouse.

"You feeling better?" I want to call him baby. I must be losing my mind.

He nods and sits down on the couch beside me. "I'll call Sheila and Betsy tomorrow and say sorry for ditching."

"That'd be good." He's so beautiful tonight—his eyes and lips swollen from crying and his cheeks blushing with residual embarrassment. I find him fascinating and distracting. And next thing I know, I'm again acting like much more than Vedie's friend. My arms are around him, and my lips are on his damp cheeks, trying to taste any salt lingering there from his tears. Tears that prove how much he cares for me. "Come to bed."

I don't have to beg. He stands up and toes off his sneakers, and as he does this, I decide that tomorrow, I'll take him to the shops in Windward to pick out an even better pair of jeweled flip-flops than the ones he lost on the beach when Joey beat him up. He steps in front of me, and I follow him to my bedroom.

I want to see him naked more than I've wanted anything in a very long time. He stands at the foot of my bed, his eyes fixed on something off to the left, and I unbutton his blouse and very slowly push it from his shoulders. The bra he wears must be made for a girl in middle school. It's thin and cotton, mint green with tiny stars on it. He probably bought it with his hard-earned dollars at a Walmart or a K-Mart, not in Victoria's Secret, where I'm sure he wishes it came from. But I think it's sexy and perfect, and I'm pretty sure Vedie knows this as my hands move to his flat chest and squeeze.

"Mateo." I wonder if it's wrong to be so crazy about the way he says my name...that's really not my name, but represents the man I become when I'm with Vedie.

"Oh, baby..." I say it. I call him by the pet name I've been thinking about all night. And it feels good, the way it drops so naturally off my tongue as if I'd called this man *baby* a thousand times before.

When he hears the endearment, he pulls me against him. My eager hands slide down his slim, lithe body, landing on the round ass that has teased me all night. My fingers slide up beneath his shorts, and I discover a little secret: Vedie's ass cheeks are bare as he's wearing a lace thong. I run a single finger beneath the elastic dividing his butt in two, and he gasps, so I do it again. And again.

"Your shorts...they have to come off..." I step back because I want to watch as he undresses for me. He shimmies out of what I consider the world's sexiest cutoffs, and here he stands in his flimsy cotton bra and a baby-pink thong. His dick is hard and ready; it fills the front of the thong, which is about the hottest thing I've ever seen. Vedie's a man in every way, but he doesn't hold back from wearing what makes him feel sexy and relaxed and authentic. "You're beautiful. I want you so much."

It hits me how capable my words are of seducing him when he gasps and again presses his smooth, brown body against me. "Well, what are you waiting for, Teo? You're not bare-assed yet," he says. I know what he wants, so I pull off my polo shirt and shorts and stand before him as he stands before me, in just my underwear.

Vedie drops to his knees in front of me and drags my briefs to my ankles. For a split second, he just breathes on me. I'm so needy I have to fight not to shove my dick into his mouth. But this moment of waiting makes what happens next the best thing I've ever felt. I'm suddenly engulfed in a warm snug eager wetness, and I find myself thanking the same distant God who turned His back on me for so many years in my youth for gifting me with this singular, spectacular pleasure.

Vedie is on fire with desire for me, and he demonstrates his enthusiasm with his strong lips and tongue. Every now and then, a brush of sharp white teeth nearly brings me to completion well before I'd planned. When I can hold back no longer, I push his head from my crotch and help him to his feet, only to lead him to my bed and push him down on his back.

"It's your turn," I say, but what I mean is, "It's my turn."

My need is all consuming as I slide the thong to the side and get my mouth onto his swollen dick while slipping my fingers beneath the elastic band separating his ass cheeks. As I climb between his knees, he pulls his dick out of the side of the thong. I'm only too eager to kiss him sweetly; I spread my tongue over the tip and listen for a gasp, which he delivers immediately. Over and over, I slide my lips up and down his length and listen to his sounds, which, again, almost push me over the edge. Then I slip a finger into my mouth and waste no time finding his body's back entrance. It's not as easy to push inside him with a damp finger as it is with a lubed one, but I do my best, and he likes it. He moans and grinds his hips into my face, and when his movements become frenzied, I say, "Let's finish this."

When I nudge his legs apart with my elbow and the side of my face, he is wide open to me, so I push my finger in a little more while at the same time sucking with everything I've got. He offers no explanation but moves my face away with his hand just before he comes. And before he's even finished, Vedie's already shoving me down on my back and taking my dick into his mouth—so far inside I worry he'll choke. But he refuses to be pushed away, and after three quick thrusts, I release deep in his throat.

We finally separate, flopping onto our backs on the bed, completely spent. I search for the right words, but they're lost to me. So I pull him onto my chest and unhook the clasp of his bra so he can be comfortable, and say, "Baby." But I want to say *my baby*.

I think I might wait and say it tomorrow, because I need to take this thing one step at a time.

Vedie hums; I can't make out the tune, but we drift away to its sweet sound.

VEDIE

We lie in bed on top of the sheets. Mateo's on his belly; I'm on my side right next to him. We're bare-assed and aren't being shy about it. I trace the raised, puckered-up skin of his back scars with my finger. And he lets me.

We don't say a thing, though. I figure these scars say it all. This man has suffered, and that's all I need to know. But he suffered at the hands of somebody who didn't have a reason. At least Marcus and Tyrone and Juan had a good reason for what they did to me—they think what I am is warped and twisted, and they wanted to fix me to be straight and narrow.

After about half an hour, Mateo flips over onto his back and stares up into my eyes. I want so bad for him to tell me what went down—how he got scars from his neck to his ass—but he doesn't offer an explanation for it and keeps running a finger over the bruises on my throat. He says, "Joey hasn't gotten what's coming to him for what he did to you."

"Did the asshole who did that shit to your back get what was coming to him?" I decide I might as well put myself out there, or I'm never going to learn one damn thing about the man beside me.

Immediately, Mateo starts sweating. His perfect cut body glazes over with a light sheen of moisture, even though he's not pumping iron on his front porch. His breathing speeds up, too. But his eyes—the color of coffee when it's swimming in cream—stay fixed on the ceiling instead of rolling back in his head. "Daniel's dead, if that's what you mean."

This isn't what I expected. "Daniel's the guy who took you?"

He nods. "Eight years after he took me, he dropped me off down the street from my house, and then he went and parked on a side street—at the very place where he grabbed me—and blew his head off."

It's hard not to gasp, but I don't. It wouldn't do either of us any good. "Think he was sorry for what he did to you?"

Mateo smiles, but it's not a happy one. "I was almost sixteen, and he knew it couldn't go on for much longer. And I think he didn't want to get caught. Child molesters don't make many friends in prison."

I nod, and then I dare to do something he forgot to do last night when he got us both off. I lean down and kiss him. His arms curve around me, and his lips start to move underneath mine, and in this kiss, there's more feeling than he ever showed me before. And I already know Mateo can't cry. I'm pretty sure he gave up on crying at some point when he was a scared little kid. He saw that bawling didn't do any good, so he stopped doing it altogether. But he's letting out his heart through this kiss.

Truth is, I've never been kissed in quite this way before. At one point, he's desperate and on fire with what I think might be anger. The kisses are sharp; they bite and they burn. And then his mouth, his face, his arms as they hold me—they all go soft. They grow almost limp, and he lets me shape the kiss with my lips and clutch him tight with my hands. He lets me set the pace until another frenzy of harsh kisses starts up again.

What's fucked up is I don't hear a voice inside me telling me I'm sweet, soft Vedie *or* bold, tough Vedie. I'm just a man kissing another man. Learning about him. Learning about me.

Mateo doesn't look at me when the kiss finally ends. He sits, slides his legs over the side of the bed, and faces the wall. Then he says in a raspy voice, "I want to take you to Windward to buy you some new sandals."

When he stands, I get another good look at the scars that cover his strong back. Must be a hundred of them there, but they blend together to look like thick ropes of raised skin. And the ass beneath that carved up back—so high and tight and ripped from all of the swimming he does. To me, Mateo is a work of art—better than the fabric picture I hung over his couch—and this art is all for me.

At least, it's mine today.

I know what I have to do. I'm going to make some art he can keep, to brighten up his cottage even when I'm long gone. "I want to buy some stuffing at the craft store. Gonna make pillows out of my two plaid skirts." His boring brown couch could sure use a touch of color. It's worth spending some of my meager savings on.

Mateo turns and stares at me. He tilts his head like I'm some kind of mystery he can't solve, when I'm really just a wide-open book, and he says, "We'll go to the craft store too. And then out to an early lunch."

The last time we were in town, the two assholes in the café almost wrecked everything. "You don't have to take me anywhere in public, you know."

He waves his hand in the air to make my words go away. "Be ready in thirty minutes."

"It'll be tough, seeing as I've got to shower, shave my legs, and do my hair and makeup."

"How does an hour sound?"

"Doable."

"I'll be on the porch with my weights. Let me know when you're done in the bathroom."

Mateo bends down and pulls some basketball shorts from a small pile of clothes on the floor, and then he's gone.

I'm left all alone, naked, except for the redness that covers my whole face from the rough kisses...and my pure joy.

I think I like it here on this island.

Maybe I'll stay a while.

Chapter Thirteen

MATT'S JOURNAL DATED MAY 2012

"Anger issues." This is what the high school guidance counselor blamed for my inability to restrain myself from punching in the face anybody who looked at me in a way I didn't like. Teachers included.

It's just that when I returned home, everything was different. I was no longer the sheltered little boy who'd lived in the biggest house on the street with the overprotective and affluent family, who was expected to follow in his father's proud footsteps and study law at Yale. That boy died eight years ago, the first time he was raped on the kitchen floor of a beat-up trailer. And I wasn't the street punk I'd turned into. At least, my mother didn't allow me to be the street punk I'd become over the next eight years. And I'll admit it now—that shit was confusing. I didn't know who to be or how to be. All I knew was I got fifteen stripes on my back if I broke into tears at Daniel's house, and so I learned to respond to every tough situation in my life with anger.

And it didn't take me long to figure out I wasn't in any way similar to the other kids at Marblehead High. Sure, all teens get into conflicts, but the street kid in me swore colorfully when intimidated and brandished his fists when threatened. Yup—I sure as hell had major "anger issues." Who could blame me?

The other students couldn't figure out why I had to be such an emo punk in their preppy world, and how on earth a sixteen-year-old freshman could barely read, and why I insisted on wearing my hair long and straggly, hanging down over my black leather jacket, even on the hot days when they were all decked out in Ralph Lauren's spring line. They were compelled to tease and taunt me.

So maybe at school, I swung first. And maybe I cursed them out with superior vulgar creativity. Maybe I got kicked out of school for pushing my Phys Ed teacher, Mr. Lawrence, up against the gymnasium wall and telling him he was dead after he laughed at me in front of the whole class because I didn't know what a double bogey was.

But maybe I still was a victim...of my own uncontrolled anger. And maybe it wasn't Mom's fault, and she actually *had* to do what she did. She'd phrased it this way: "Matthew, dear, I have no choice but to send you to a boarding school where they can deal effectively with your unsuitable behaviors, because the Lord knows, I can't."

And so I was sent away again.

At first, I thought I was being punished for surviving the only way I knew how—by using my foul mouth and quick fists—but maybe it was for the best I got shipped off to school. It's easy to admit that now, years after the icy slam of my mother's rejection. But at the

Englewood School for (fucking wayward) Boys, I learned how to behave and control myself. I gained all the knowledge of the school subjects I'd missed in my years with Daniel. In fact, I excelled at these things. I lost the piercings and the leather jacket and smoking and drinking habits and all outward signs of a delinquent attitude.

And I lost any desire to have even the most remote connection with other human beings. I realized that if people weren't literally fucking me, they were thinking of ways to fuck me over.

So here I sit on my sunny beach—a dozen years free of Daniel and seven years free of everyone else—surrounded by furry friends who can't leave me if they want to eat today. I don't know if I still suffer from anger issues because I never put myself in a position where I could possibly get angry. I mean, how angry can I really get at a cat or an employer I only have to deal with online or the girl who brings me my grilled chicken Caesar salad at The Only Tiki Hut on Placida Island?

MATT

"You aren't really a girl."

What the fuck? A ten-year-old-kid in the polyester stuffing aisle at Landon's Craft Shop clearly feels he has the right, or the obligation, to inform Vedie that he isn't "passing" as a woman.

"You're right, genius; I ain't *only* a girl. There's a bit of boy sprinkled in me, just in case I want to pee standing up."

Sometimes I doubt Vedie can take care of himself, and then I realize in some ways, he surely can.

"Ain't is not a word. You said it, so that makes you a dummy *and* not a girl!" The little boy stands in the middle of the aisle, staring at Vedie's dress with condemnation.

Vedie ignores the kid's last insult and continues to paw through the bags of stuffing, squeezing each one in search of the perfect filling for the throw pillows he plans to make. It doesn't take long for the boy's mother to show up. "Will, you know you're not supposed to talk to strangers." She eyes Vedie critically. "And you, sir, do not belong anywhere near children. They're not safe with your kind."

I expect Vedie's eyes to fill up, but surprisingly, they don't. In fact, he doesn't even look away from the stuffing bags as he says, "You don't have nothing to worry about with me, ma'am. I'm not interested in your kid."

As the woman scowls, grasps her little boy by the hand, and drags him down the aisle, it crosses my mind that Vedie could never be cruel and dangerous to a small boy the way Daniel had been to me. And ironically, Daniel had been the picture of "normal" with his closely clipped dark hair and librarian-looking glasses and button-down shirts. One could argue that Vedie appears to be anything but "normal" with his rainbow-colored minidress and black leggings, red lipstick, and scruffy beard, but I'm starting to realize "normal" isn't all that relevant, especially when it comes to relationships.

And my anger issues certainly aren't "normal." The prickly heat of annoyance rises to the surface of my skin, and it turns quickly into outright fury. Before I've thought it through, I'm stalking down the aisle after the nasty woman. When I get to her side, I say, "You have no right to accuse him of behaving improperly."

The woman turns toward me and replies, "*Him?* Are you sure he's a man?"

"You thrive on tearing people apart, don't you, lady?" I look down at the little boy's wide eyes. "You ought to take a lesson from him." I point to Vedie, who's staring at me with his mouth hanging open. "He wouldn't hurt you or your mother or even a fly to save his life—"

"Mateo!" Vedie calls out, and soon he's beside me, grabbing my arm and dragging me away, much like the mother did to her son a few minutes ago.

"I'm not about to let them drive us out of this store! Vedie, you came here for a reason, and I'm going to see to it that you get what you want."

Is this really me? I thought I left Mr. Confrontational behind in high school.

Vedie stops walking and pushes on my shoulders with both hands so I have to focus on him. "What I don't want is to cause a major scene."

"That woman and her rude kid were out of line!"

As my voice increases in volume, Vedie's grows softer. He almost sounds like a patient kindergarten teacher. "Mateo, the world divides people up into male and female— and most folks can only see those two categories. I'm not a perfect match for either, so I show myself to the world as a messed-up blend of both. It makes sense that I live my life expecting trouble and trying my best to ignore assholes."

"But you don't have to be a victim. You have rights— why don't you stand up for them?" I know immediately that I've asked the wrong question. In fact, I asked an unfair question, like the one everybody used to ask me about why I didn't leave Daniel when I had a chance. In any case, I already know the answer, and it's the same as the answer that took me years to acknowledge. What it comes down to is simple fear; Vedie's doing what he thinks offers him the best chance of survival.

In the same way, I stuck with Daniel because I thought it was my best chance at staying alive.

"I've been on the wrong end of hate crimes one too many times, so I pretty much always hold the fear of getting my ass kicked in the back of my head. See, people don't like it that I can't fit inside one of the gender boxes—it scares them bad. I fuck with their idea of what it means to be a man. And then being black *and* stuck in the middle of the gender boxes, well, it's no picnic, dude."

"But it isn't right."

"Don't I know it? I think the world's changing for the better, Teo, but it's not changing fast enough. So I've got to try and be cool with folks who piss on me, and hope they'll end up seeing I'm a person, just the same as them."

I look down at my sneakers and then at Vedie's. "Let's go get you a new pair of sandals. With jewels on top...and lots of them."

"Shopping therapy works for me. But I wanted to make some pillows for the couch... I guess getting a couple yards of rainbow cheetah stretch velvet isn't worth having security come and escort me out of the store." Vedie shrugs and glances toward the door, speaking again without realizing he's thinking aloud. "I decided I'm gonna use my plaid skirts to make throw pillows for the bed, but then there's your plain brown couch that needs a touch of brightness too."

"We'll come back here after we finish up at the shoe store. And you've got to stop cutting up your clothes to make household decorations, or you'll end up walking around the house stark naked." I smile because that might actually be nice. Without thinking, I take his hand in mine. "Come on, Vedie, let's go get you some sandals that work better with your outfit than those high-tops."

Chapter Fourteen

MATT

I haven't disassociated in weeks.

And it's not as if I haven't faced anything tough that would normally send my spirit rocketing out of my body to the safety of a distorted perspective from ten feet above. I've dealt with making friendships—a completely new experience. I've accepted that another human being needs me, and I've learned to like it. I've directly addressed Vedie's conflicts and felt rage on his behalf, and not faded away. But the most daunting undertaking—one I never thought I'd allow—is I've let myself care about another person.

I'm stretched out in bed, and Vedie is sprawled, without inhibition, over the entire left side of my body. It's after nine in the morning—well past the time I should be pumping iron and acting as if I wouldn't rather be right here. I wait without a trace of apprehension to see which side of Vedie will open his eyes. I would never have guessed when I finally opened my heart enough to let a person in, it would be a physical male who fluctuates easily in the way he expresses his gender. And never, ever would I have imagined this really wouldn't matter to me.

His left eye pops open. "Are you staring at me? It isn't polite to stare."

"I can't help it—you're easy on the eyes."

"Want a taste of this eye candy, Teo?"

"More than you know." I lean over to kiss him and find myself wondering how this happened to my life.

After a kiss I don't want to end reaches its conclusion, he sighs softly. "It's been almost two weeks since…you know, since that thing went down on the beach." His hands move to his throat.

He has never admitted what we both know to be true—Joey was the one who tried to choke him, not to mention drown him, on the beach, leaving his throat bruised and scratched.

"Yeah…almost."

"I think I'm ready to go back to work."

"No." I can't even tolerate the suggestion. "Not until you go to the cops." My shoulders become rigid, and I'm not sure whether to hold him tighter or push him away. "It isn't safe, Vedie, and we both know it." Pulling him tightly against me wins out.

"I can't live off of you forever. I've got to work so you won't be stuck feeding me and buying me clothes and shit."

"It's not a problem to feed you or to help you out in other ways, and I like having you around." I hope I'm successfully hiding that I've never been happier in my life. "But if you're itching to go back to work, let's head over to the police station to report what happened to you."

Vedie stretches and climbs from the bed. "Can we swing by the Tiki Hut before we go to the cops, so I can talk to Angie? You know, to make sure there's still a job waiting for me there."

I nod because he's meeting me halfway.

"Cool. I'll go get ready." He slips out of bed and strolls naked to the doorway, stopping to grab athletic shorts and a T-shirt from his bin.

I have a feeling I've seen the last of the softer side of Vedie, at least until this problem has been handled.

"JOEY HASN'T BEEN around in almost two weeks." Angie barely looks up from the receipts she's organizing at the bar. "I lost Joey on the very same day I lost you, Vedie—but he didn't have the good grace to give me a call and let me know he was done here. Two workers no-showed in one day—yeah, it's been a difficult couple of weeks. I've been shorthanded."

Vedie glances up at me like he's seeking my permission to ask if his job is still available, so I give it to him with a nod. "You still need me as a busboy?"

Finally, Angie puts the receipts down on the bar and looks up at him. "You left me high and dry."

"I'm sorry."

"It had better not become a habit."

"It's not gonna."

"Then be here for dinner tomorrow night and plan to work your butt off." And boom, Angie's attention is back on the paperwork.

"Thanks, Angie." Vedie grabs my arm and pulls me from the bar. "Come on, Mateo."

As we walk back to my truck, I can't stop myself from saying something. "Just because Joey is gone right now doesn't mean he's going to stay gone. You still need to go to the police." We seem to have arrived at a mutual, but unspoken, understanding that it was Joey who harmed Vedie. I unlock the truck and open the passenger door for him.

"You worry way too much." He flashes me one of his best grins. "I'm not gonna waste the rest of my last day off work filling out papers at the police station, big dawg. Let's do something fun with the day." He slides into the truck and looks my way, as if to dare me to challenge him.

"Let's do fun stuff *after* you've filed a complaint on Joey." I walk around the car once I've made my suggestion.

By the time I hop into the driver's seat, Vedie is ready with his distraction. "I've got some cash saved up, and now that I'm gonna be working again, I say we spend some of it. So I'm thinking we oughta head for the mainland. Heard there was a horseback riding place in Tully. It'll be my treat!"

"I've never ridden a horse." A senseless comment on my part, but it breaks the tension about the Joey issue. And I think I just let Vedie off the hook.

"That makes two of us." He buckles in and adds, "The horse ranch is on Old Route 302." He leans toward me and takes my hand. "Can't wait to see my man on the back of a horse."

He just referred to me as his man. *Is that what I am?* I scratch my head, smile, and say, "Route 302 it is then."

MATT'S JOURNAL DATED MARCH 2013

Once I'd been living with my parents for a while, I felt as if I had to take back control of my life, which falsely implies I actually had some control when I lived with Daniel. When it came to the important things like whose bed I slept in, it's true I didn't. But with the small stuff—where I hung out after school, if it was time for another piercing, whether or not I did my homework, what I filled my face with—I'd been completely on my own. I'd been living in the land of "anything goes."

I resented some of the changes. My parents seemed to want to change me into who I would have been had I not been abducted and held for eight long, formative years. But I had been taken, and a different Matthew was the result.

And this Matthew had to take back control.

In therapy, I was told I had some rights. I had the right to experience my own feelings and the right to feel safe. I was told I could let people know what I needed, and in theory, they'd see that I got it. I had the right to my own personal space and to tell people no. I had the right to the privacy of my story. And I had the right to make choices.

Mom dutifully drove me back and forth to the appointments with my psychologist who told me all these things that should happen, and she and Dad even joined me in some sessions, always nodding sympathetically, but I was never granted any of the rights I'd been promised.

Mom told me precisely how to feel; Dad informed me I was now safe and not to question it—end of story. If I asked for time alone in my room, I was told it was unhealthy for me to cloister myself upstairs night and day, and I should be downstairs interacting with the family. I had the right to say no, but whenever I did, Mom cried and Dad turned on his heel and walked away. I was expected to share my story with counselors and family friends and, hardest of all, with my parents. Talking about the details of how I'd been regularly raped by a grown man since I was seven, and the way that made me feel, was not something I could make myself do.

All of this amounted to me having zero power to make choices.

My days of being a victim were over, so I started to act out. When "no, thank you" didn't work, it shifted into "hell no!" Which worked a lot better. When "I'd like to spend some time in my room" had no effect, "leave me the fuck alone" did.

Instead of rebuilding bonds, I became further alienated from my family and entered a world where nobody could tell me what to do.

I find it hard, even now, to get out of the "you're not the boss of me" frame of mind. Being in complete charge, never compromising, and following the "my way or the highway" approach, have made it a requirement that I live alone and limit all human interaction.

VEDIE

"I got this tired old mare, and Mateo got this raging stallion...and I'm not joking."

"Did you ride on trails through the woods?" Betsy must be super into horses because she seems real interested in our horseback ride.

"Even better. We drove to the beach and rode the horses along the shoreline," Mateo says, winking at me. "We tried to get the horses to walk side by side, but they refused. Darth, my horse, followed Sally, Vedie's horse, a couple miles down the coast and back."

I have to smile because Mateo's sure come a long way since the day I first came onto him in the tiki bar. The dude was a total loner back then—it was just him and his four cats against the world—and now, he's got me and some friends, too. "Maybe it was fun for you, but your horse kept on biting mine in the hindquarters. Sally didn't like it at all—she nearly sent me flying at least ten times!"

"Ha! Wish I could've been there to see that."

I'm not pissed off at Betsy for teasing me anymore, so I laugh.

The best idea hits my brain. "Sheila, are you off work on Sunday?"

"I'm on the schedule for brunch, but I should be finished by two. Three, at the latest."

"All four of us could go back to the beach and ride." My three favorite people and me riding horses along the beach is a perfect plan. "But this time, Mateo's gonna get Sally."

"A second horseback ride sounds like fun, but I think you'd break old Sally's heart if you turned your back on her, Vedie," Mateo says, playing along.

Sheila brings us back to our picnic on the beach behind Mateo's cottage. "You've got the best place here, Matt."

"You've also got a very lucky houseguest," Betsy adds. "Pass the pumpkin bread, huh?"

I reach over Mateo and grab the basket of bread I baked. "I'm not gonna deny it; I'm a lucky little shit." When I hand off the bread to Betsy, Mateo catches my hand midair and pulls it to his face, and then presses it to his scruffy cheek. And I get misty because it's not the kind of thing a guy like Mateo would do unless he meant for me to know that somehow I'm his.

"Almost time for swimming, Betz?" Sheila bails me out. "It's getting hot on this beach." She grabs ahold of Betsy's hand, and even though Betsy's still chomping on pumpkin bread, she lets herself get dragged down to the water.

Mateo's still pressing my hand to his cheek and looking at me with a soft expression. I'm not one to get tongue-tied too much, but I can't think of a thing to say.

"You're lost in thought, Vedie." He finally lets go of my hand. I have to do something with it because it's tingling, so I straighten the waistband of my Speedo.

"I have to clean up from lunch. You go get in the water with those two." We look over at Sheila and Betsy who're nuzzling each other, waist-deep in the ocean.

"I think they've got things well in hand without me," he replies, and I can't miss that he's still looking at me so sweet. He pushes me down so I'm flat on my back on the picnic blanket.

"Don't blame me if the potato salad spoils—"

His lips are on mine before I finish the sentence, and it's all good.

Chapter Fifteen

VEDIE

"Well, hello, Vedie. Isn't that your name?"

"Yes, dear, his name is Vedie." Mrs. North glances real quick at her husband and goes back to gawking at me. "I certainly didn't expect to find you here...with Matthew." She looks around the kitchen. I do too because I'm worried about what proof Mateo's mom might notice and realize that I live here now.

"Yeah...um, how about you guys come on in?" Mrs. N pushes right past me. "I'll go get Mateo. He's in the bedroom and...uh...I'll be right back, ma'am."

She makes this huffing sound and mutters, "Robert, why on earth are you still standing out on the porch? Come inside."

I head to the bedroom as fast as a roach races for the cookie crumbs.

Mateo's hanging the newest piece of artwork I made over the bed so we can look at it when we first wake up. It's a mobile made from all sorts of stuff I found on the beach behind the cottage. Everything's dangling from old shoelaces off a couple of wire coat hangers I twisted together and painted a color called melon ball. Mateo's wrestling with my mobile right now; some of the strings are long, so he's got a shell in his face and a kid's plastic shovel banging on his ear.

"Teo...uh, Teo...we've got visitors." I say it real blunt, figuring he'll know who's here.

"Are there squirrels on the bird feeder again?"

"Human visitors, dude."

He lets go of the mobile, and it falls to the bed, but I'm not mad because I know he's freaking out. "My parents..."

That's all he says before he goes blank and drops to the bed right next to my tangled mobile.

"Teo, you can handle this." *But can I?*

I've got to do some quick thinking. First off, I take a look at what I'm wearing, not wanting to give away my gender confusion to Mateo's folks, especially when he's in no condition to discuss it. I breathe a sigh of relief because I'm wearing light-blue cotton pajama pants and one of Mateo's oversized white T-shirts. Hope to hell my hot-pink and lime-green polka-dotted toenails didn't catch their attention back in the kitchen.

I stuff my feet into my high-tops and head back out to the kitchen. "Mateo's getting dressed, and he asked me to make you some tea, so please take a load off..." I point to the kitchen chairs. "I think I'll make us blueberry tea I picked it up at the—"

"Just. Get. Matthew." Mrs. N's face is set like stone. "Or I'll go get him myself."

"Of course. I'll get him now." I race off to the bedroom where Mateo seems to be back in the here and now. "Dude, your mom wants to see you right now. She's not gonna wait until you're up for it." I decide to get dressed in an outfit that can't possibly be confused for girl's clothes. Explaining we're gay to his parents is one thing, but explaining to them their son's lover has a tough time choosing whether to be a dude or a lady is totally another.

"I'm not ready to face them." This is one of the most honest confessions he's ever made, but we've got no time to celebrate.

"*You* don't have to face them, Teo. *We're* gonna face them together. And it's gonna be fine." I grab his hand and pull him to his feet. He shouldn't go out there without a shirt on, so I go to his chest of drawers and pull out a striped polo he looks nice in. "Put this on."

He throws the shirt over his head, but he doesn't look preppy-cool quite yet.

"Here." I hand him an elastic band from off my wrist. "Tie your hair back."

He does as I ask without a question.

"Now, we've got to plan our story."

"Our story?" The man is clueless.

"We're gonna tell them I'm staying here until...until my apartment's been fumigated on account of a bad case of roaches."

"*What?*" Mateo sends me a look; he thinks I'm batshit crazy. But I can work with it—it's an expression and not a blank face.

"Yup. Fumigated. Your folks aren't ready to learn we're living together." The thought makes me giggle. "So we're not 'living together.' You're helping out a friend in need."

He shrugs. "That's not a lie, is it?"

I feel as if he kicked me. "No. I guess it's not a lie." I swallow hard and say, "Now, go on out there before your mama barges in here and finds my nighty hanging from the mirror."

Mateo's eyes don't roll back like usual. They turn steely as he passes by me and heads to the kitchen. I stand in the bedroom doorway, peek around the corner, and listen.

"Mom, Dad. So glad you stopped by." They don't hug or kiss; they stand on either end of the kitchen table and stare at each other. "But you really should've called."

"Why, Matthew? Are you embarrassed that your cottage has become a gay love nest?"

"Christ, Mom..."

He was doing so well. I hope to hell her nasty-ass comment won't change things.

"Lily...we didn't come here to pick a fight with our son. We're here to visit."

Mrs. N sniffs. "All right, all right. But does that...that *boy* have to spend the day with us? I don't feel comfortable with him."

I scramble back to the bedroom and close the door as quiet as I can. *It's happening again*, I think. *I don't seem normal to even more people in the world*. They don't even give me a chance because I'm not like them. Even Mateo's parents can tell I'm not a regular man.

I push the "fun-on-the-beach" mobile off the bed, and it crashes to the floor. What a dumbass project; I'd hoped it would make us think about good things in life like beach fun, every morning right when we open our eyes. But what kind of loser collects trash on a beach and hangs it off a couple coat hangers and calls it art? My kind of loser, that's who.

I feel tired and alone. And I'm always going to be tired and alone.

It's so easy to close my eyes and fall asleep in the narrow strip of sunlight shining in through the window on Matthews's big bed.

I WAKE UP to Mateo shaking me real gentle by the shoulders. "Vedie...Vedie..."

"Teo? Why aren't you visiting with your folks?"

"Because you promised you'd be with me. That we'd do this together. And you never came back to the kitchen."

"But I don't think your mama wants me."

Mateo leans down and hugs me, then whispers into my ear. "What about what *I* want?"

I sit up in the bed. "What *do* you want?"

"I want my best friend to come to the Tiki Hut and have lunch with my parents and me."

"In that case, I guess I'll get dressed."

Mateo wants me.

A WHOLE LUNCH is plenty of time for Mrs. N to size up Mateo and me. At first, she pretends I'm not here; she refuses to look at me. We're sitting in the best seats at The Only Tiki Hut—down by the shore under an enormous yellow umbrella—thanks to Sheila telling Angie we're VIPs today. Mrs. N's got this floppy straw hat on I kind of wish was mine, and the coolest Prada sunglasses that must've cost a friggin' mint. But we don't talk fashion. We don't talk at all, and she even lets Mr. North start the conversation. I'm pretty sure it's because she wants to figure out her angle. As in, how she's going to attack us.

"How's business, Matthew? Have you held onto all of your accounts?"

Mateo doesn't have a problem talking business with his dad. "Yeah, I've kept all of my accounts and added a couple. Word spread in the business world that my work increases profitability, and so—"

"I'm surprised you haven't lost your focus." Mrs. N chimes in and glances over at me, then makes that I'm-smelling-shit face.

"No, Mom. I will admit to spending less time at my computer since I've been with Vedie, but I've been more focused when I'm working, so my productivity is up."

"That's good news, Matthew. We wondered when you were going to start living." Mr. N isn't the sharpest tool in the shed when it comes to dealing with his messed-up son, but he's more clueless than mean.

And Mateo's mind doesn't disappear from the beach. "My life has been more balanced lately." He smiles at me, and his folks don't miss it.

"We had hoped to be alone with you when we discussed this matter, but since *that* apparently isn't going to happen...well, we are forced to raise the issue in the presence of a stranger." She says the word so *stranger* is the loudest part. "Your father and I are concerned that Daniel's long-term effect on you has led you to believe you are homosexual. Or that Daniel somehow changed your sexuality by...by those things he did to you."

If Mateo is going to cut and run, he's going to do it right about now. I study his eyes, but they don't flicker and roll back.

"It doesn't work that way, Mom."

"What are you talking about?"

"My sexuality is *my* sexuality. Sexual assault did not cause my orientation to change."

"Matthew, I hate to be blunt, but, under the circumstances, I have no choice." She doesn't look uncomfortable at all. She looks hell-bent. "Just say, for example, you enjoyed some of the...sexual interactions... between you and Daniel. You may have become confused... and assumed you are homosexual."

I grab my water glass and suck down half because I have to do something with my mouth to stop me from cursing her out. Mr. N is on the same wavelength as me. He coughs a couple times and then gulps down his iced tea.

Mateo's eyes are dim, and the lids have closed halfway. I think, *this isn't good.* But he breathes deep and swallows with a loud gulping sound and tells her, "I never was gay, Mom. But I never was straight either. In fact, my sexual orientation would be very difficult to describe to a person like you, who only see two choices—gay or straight."

At the same time, Mrs. N says, "That's because the only two choices are heterosexual and homosexual," Mr. N says, "But try us."

"I'm attracted to *people*, Mom, not to genders. It wouldn't matter if Vedie were a man or a woman, gay or straight. It's who he is inside that intrigues and attracts me."

Mateo hasn't ever told me this shit before. But then, I never asked. And Mr. N is nodding as if he gets it. Mrs. N isn't as cool with it, but I think she heard what he said too.

"So am I to expect that your father and I will never have grandchildren from you?"

I want to ask who the fuckin' hell she thinks she is, asking her son that kind of question. But instead, I reach my hand under the table and squeeze Mateo's knee. "We're not ready to talk about having kids, ma'am," I say.

"But two men... All I'm saying is children aren't really a possibility, are they? At least not biological children." She looks damn smug, like she's proved some bizarro point.

"I think your question is somewhat premature, Mom." Mateo doesn't grab my hand and squeeze it back. Instead, he flags down Sheila and says, "It's time to order."

Mrs. N is quiet throughout the rest of our lunch. She watches real close how me and Mateo look at each other and laugh together. And Mateo even tells his folks about how fun it was to go horseback riding on the beach with Sheila and Betsy.

When we get served frozen strawberry margaritas for a liquid dessert, his mom finally speaks up. "Well, this Vedie person isn't exactly the one I'd have chosen for you, but you seem to be happy enough, Matthew." She still refuses to look my way. On the bright side, she referred to me as an actual human being.

Mr. N says, "I think this is the best margarita I've ever tasted."

MATT'S JOURNAL DATED AUGUST 2014

"You know you wanted it."

When I got a little bit older, this is what Daniel said to keep me in line. To stop me from complaining too much or telling someone about us, he insisted that I enjoyed what happened in his bed. But I didn't enjoy it—I despised it—though sometimes my body betrayed me. When he touched me in certain ways, I just couldn't stop the physical reaction, but, shit, I tried like hell. This might have been the worst part of the abuse: How it fucked with my head. I felt as if I was a partner in crime; part of me believed him when he said I asked for it.

I understand now that no child can be a true partner in anything sexual with an adult. I was his victim, plain and simple. And thankfully, this realization sank in by the time I was eighteen. But thinking of myself as a sexual victim whose body responded to the advances of my abuser still made me wonder how much control I had.

And then, for years, I agonized over my sexual orientation. *Was I gay?* Some of what Daniel did to me felt good. *Was I straight?* I appreciated the way girls looked and acted and, on the rare occasion I got within a few feet of them, I liked the way they smelled. By the time I finished college, I'd succeeded in having a series of stressful and relatively unsatisfying one-night stands and several awkward dates with women, but zero relationships.

I still don't know why I couldn't get into it with those women. Back then, I figured probably I *was* gay. Now, eight years into my life as a recluse, I realize it wasn't my sexuality that held me back; it was that I was broken.

How could I participate in a relationship of any sort—gay, straight, or even simple friendship—when it was all I could do to make it through the day on my own?

I'm fine with my solitary life. I kind of have to be, since I can't relax if I'm not alone. For eight years under Daniel's roof, I lived on edge—always wondering when he'd be home and what he'd want of me. I'm not about to revisit that hell.

But every once in a while, like now, when I'm sitting on the beach looking out over the water, I wish someone were sitting beside me.

Chapter Sixteen

MATT

What's made me stronger lately is how I've been helping Vedie in his struggle with Joey—by standing up for him in public and taking care of him at my home. I've given myself full credit for my newfound ability to cope with Vedie's challenges and to respond in the ways he needs. The look in his eyes each time I've stepped in and "saved" him—an expression of disbelief, combined with awe, thankfulness, and relief—feeds into a new "capable" self-image that has suddenly emerged after years of absence. But it's more than that; I think Vedie's presence—reassuring, nonjudgmental, and optimistic—is also a major factor in my new outlook.

And this realization has me reeling.

I'm ready to accept I've progressed, very suddenly and radically, in the direction of positive human interaction. And I'm comfortable with the idea that Vedie's neediness draws from me a response of strength. But the idea that his very presence has moved me in a direction of emotional normalcy—of my finally being fixed—well, this I cannot accept.

"You got a messed-up look on your face, Mateo."

We're sitting at the kitchen table, talking about how dinner with my parents went far better than anticipated by either of us.

"I'm not sure what you mean, Vedie."

"You've got a scared face. What's up with that, huh?"

He's always invariably and brutally honest, but still I protest. "I'm fine, and your imagination is working overtime."

His eyes linger on my face for another moment, and then he shrugs. "Whatever you say, big dawg."

He toes off his high-tops and steps to the sink to rinse our breakfast dishes.

"You don't have to always be working around here, you know," I say. It sounds like an accusation.

"I was meaning to talk to you about that very thing." He turns around and faces me. "Now that I'm back to work, I think it's time I forked over some cash each month for room and board."

"No. Not necessary." His suggestion irritates me. "You keep on working and saving up your money. Having savings will give you stability...*and independence.*"

Vedie gazes directly into my eyes, injured. Having me bring up the topic of his independence from me is not what he wants. He wants to talk about "us" and how we are a unit of some sort. He hasn't yet accepted that, although I can be something of a friend and helper and a now-and-then lover, I cannot be a full partner. I can, however, change his train of thought and bring him around to feeling happy again. "When you were at work yesterday, I picked up something for you at the craft shop."

"You were supposed to be working at your computer while I was bussing tables at the Tiki Hut." His wounded expression changes into an intrigued one. He is in some ways like a child, and in many ways, so am I. But where I'm a guarded, wary, and sullen teenager, he is a thrilled and lively seven-year-old.

"What did you get me?" His voice is breathy.

"Come to the bedroom and see." Briefly, apprehension shows in tiny lines on Vedie's forehead, perhaps because I suggested the surprise was in the bedroom, and he "isn't a ho" as he's instructed me so many times before. "I hid the bags from the craft shop underneath the bed."

The worry lines vanish. I follow him as he races to the bedroom, skids to a stop, drops to his knees, and within a second, is pulling the plastic Landon's Craft Shop bags out from under the bed. He spills the contents of the bags on the tan bedspread that now sports three vibrant plaid throw pillows shaped like Tootsie Rolls, and declares, "These are candle-making supplies, or my name isn't Vedie Wilson!"

I can't stop my grin when I see his.

"Can I make them now?"

"Of course you can." I try to act casual, crossing my arms and taking a cool step away from the bed, but it's difficult to contain myself. His enthusiasm is quite contagious.

He grabs all the supplies and heads for the kitchen.

It's going to be a long, wax-filled afternoon, I think, still grinning like a fool.

THE ROMANTIC MOOD in my bedroom is definitely enhanced by the lopsided, mauve candlesticks that flicker warmly on my windowsill, bureau, and bedside table. Vedie patiently dipped and then pressed the candles into the largest shells he could find on the beach. He has an intuition for how to use small things to make big changes: candles and pillows, curtains and wall hangings, a primitive mobile hanging over my bed, as well as herbal teas and home-cooked meals. In this way, he has made my bare house feel like a real home.

I've actually never before witnessed this sort of passion for the small details of life. Until now, I've kept my existence clutter-free: no decorative ornaments or vibrant colors or stirring scents or soft fabrics to encourage my sensitivity. I've clung to a life that is plain and simple and noninspirational, which doesn't require me to reach deep into my withered heart and sift through all the dust there in search of long-ago discarded feelings.

But it's different lately. And with the homey scent of a chicken and green bean casserole baking in the oven, the glow from the candles cutting through the early-evening dimness, and a long, slim man stretched out in my bed, with eyes inviting me to join him, everything seems different.

"What are ya waiting for, Teo?" His soft voice coaxes me in ways that his eyes alone can't. "I'm getting lonely on this bed." He pats the place beside him, and I fly there. Everything is different now, including me.

"I want you, Vedie." My voice is even breathier than his. I'm indescribably thankful I'm already naked.

"I know you do, and I don't plan to make you wait." First, his arms envelop me, and then he crawls onto my chest. I'm feeling turned on, not awkward. There's no fear in my heart, just desire.

I see a new expression in his eyes. It seems to be something beyond want and even need. I immediately close my eyes so I don't have to absorb its meaning.

And tonight, he takes charge. He starts by sliding his body down my thighs and, with urgency, taking me into his mouth and keeping me there until I'm standing tall with need. When he pushes on my side, hard enough so I flip onto my belly, I know it's going to be a different kind of night.

This will be the first time a man has made love to me. No, it's not the first time a man has been inside my body, because Daniel had sex with me hundreds, possibly thousands, of times. But since Daniel, and until Vedie, there were only women.

He's in a hurry. His hands are on my ass, rubbing and squeezing, and within a minute, he's prepping me to receive him. I wait for the fear—for the memories of the suffering I've experienced—to overtake me, but it doesn't. Because it's different now.

I'm with Vedie.

He rises to his knees and there is the rumple of plastic. He moans softly as he unrolls a condom on his dick. And without further hesitation, he helps me to my knees, lines himself up behind me, and pushes. My body does not make the act of entering easy for him. It's as if my ass fights to remain in its long-untouched state. But with equal diligence, Vedie works to get in. And at the moment of his victory, I gasp, as does he. Both of us are genuinely surprised he has joined with me in this way.

I'm overwhelmed with the enormity of the sensation and so glad he can't see my face. I'm also glad I can't see his. But we don't need to look into each other's eyes to know the intensity of our bond. And when he begins to move inside me with more purpose, I experience an instinctive urge to slide out from beneath him and run away screaming. Being taken in this manner never brought me anything except pain and misery. But instead, I inexplicably push my ass back against him.

"Mateo..." The way he says my name holds me in place.

And then his hand is on my dick, and it moves with a new determination to reach his ultimate goal, our mutual satisfaction.

"I'm close, Vedie. I'm so close..."

How can I be so close to release after barely ten strokes of his hand?

Vedie is close, too. He moves in and out of me with short jerky thrusts. "Mateo...you've changed...everything...for me."

His words barely register in my frantic mind, but my body knows better—my spine stiffens with the impending doom, as certain as the ecstasy.

I'm on the brink of coming, which also surprises me as I'm in a far more submissive position than I've ever known as an adult. My willingness to be pleasured in this manner has me caught in a snare more powerful than the pleasure, itself. In those few precious and tense seconds of waiting—when I'm helpless and vulnerable, my heart as open as my body—all I can do is take what Vedie gives me.

And Vedie gives me words. "I love you, Teo. I'm in love with you."

It's beyond the point where my orgasm can be stopped.

I come into his hand as he comes inside my body.

And then, all of me, right down to the tiniest speck, retreats. I'm not sure what happens to Vedie.

WHEN I REGAIN awareness, I'm lying flat on my back on the bed. The room is dark; the mobile jangles softly. The window is wide open, and warm air blowing in from the ocean alerts me to an escape, should I need one.

Was the window open before, when I needed so badly to flee? I don't remember. At that point, all I could smell in the air was Vedie's casserole, and all I could feel on my skin was Vedie.

"Vedie," I say his name, although I'm instinctively aware he's no longer in the room. I have no idea how long

I've been lost in my mind. I don't know if I hurt him with my retreat upon his sweet declaration. I don't know if I care.

All I know is I can't love him back.

VEDIE

Curled on my side, alone on the couch—not because I'm pissed off at Mateo or anything—I just need space.

I'm trying my damnedest to fall asleep so I don't have to think about what I said and what Mateo didn't say. And how he freaked out and split in half, his body beneath me on the bed and his mind floating somewhere up near the ceiling, all because I said I was in love with him.

And right after he left his body and me on the bed, my harder side pushed every last scrap of softness in me away. It didn't say *let me handle this for you, dear*. It just shoved everything soft and sweet and gentle about me out of the way so it could take the pain. And I know women can take pain as well as men, probably better, but in me, my gentlemanly side protects my ladylike side. It knows better than to let my sensitivity get crushed.

My innermost thoughts are not always politically correct.

I screwed up. I screwed up big time. But then again, maybe not so much. All I did was admit how I felt, and that's not a crime. I pretty much always express my truth, so I'm not going to wish I could take it back now. I'm going to go to sleep and wake up tomorrow and see what the day holds for me.

I'm going to think about moving on from this cottage and from this man I sure as shit love, but who can't or don't or won't love me back. But I'm not going to do it just yet. I'm not ready to go yet.

Mateo doesn't love me, this I can see, but the fact is, he doesn't hate me either, and he treats me good enough. Mateo doesn't ever beat me or try to change me—plus, he's kind. He gets into making me feel safe, and he does all sorts of shit just to see me smile. Even if he's not in love with me, he's my friend.

Only thing is, when you love somebody, being his friend isn't enough. Being Mateo's friend is a lot like getting stuck with a knife in my heart.

I'll close my eyes and focus on tomorrow and whatever comes next. It's what I always do. Life hasn't been easy for me so far; don't know why I expected a knight in shining armor to show up and whisk me away from all of the bullshit.

But I've got a friend in Mateo, and it's more than I ever had before.

As long as I'm here, it has to be enough.

MATT

"I'll pick you up tonight. About seven, right?" I dip my head down so I can see his eyes. He hasn't been the same since we made love the night before last, when he gave me a gift I couldn't give back to him. He's defeated in a profound way I can't, or maybe I refuse to understand. And I won't lie; I'm concerned.

He hops out of the passenger seat and turns back to look at me. He isn't playful and calling me *big dawg*. "I'm gonna go to Sheila's house tonight. *Girls'* night sleepover." He says it with sarcasm, and I'm not sure why.

"Does Sheila know about this?"

He smiles, but it's colder than I'm used to.

"She invited me." He lifts his backpack from the seat. It's filled with more stuff than usual, which makes me wonder if he's planning to stay away longer than one night. My stomach and my chest and my throat tighten up, but I do my best to ignore it. "My shift tomorrow night is over at ten, if you want to pick me up then."

"Okay, Vedie." I breathe a sigh of relief and do my best to offer him a smile in return, but I fail. All I can think about is that tonight I'm going to be alone, and while I should be relieved, it's as if I'm losing something.

Or as if I'm losing *someone*.

Vedie leans into the passenger window of the truck. "Have a good night." He doesn't stand and walk away; he continues to look at me steadily. "I meant what I said, you know, Teo."

I so badly want to hear him say he loves me again. "What do you mean?" Maybe I'm fishing...*maybe I am*.

"I love you. I really can't help it." His eyes slide off to the side as if he's sorry and possibly even ashamed to have voiced his strong feelings for me again without a hint of reciprocation. Before I have a chance to say anything in response, he straightens up, slings his leopard-print backpack across his back, and turns toward the restaurant. I tell myself it's a good thing he's walking away. I don't have the right words to say at this moment.

But I'm starting to understand what it means to be your own worst enemy.

AT THE COTTAGE, I grab a big towel straight from the dryer and stroll down to the beach. There's no better place to think than this. I spread the towel on the sand, stretch out on my stomach, and let the sun soak into the scars on my back. Scars Vedie touched and related to, because he understands the devastation of my soul that accompanies them.

I'm lost in a way that brings to mind being a boy at Daniel's house. I still have no one to turn to so I can unload some of the pain and confusion weighing me down and separating me from the world. And just like I took the blame for having been ruined by Daniel, I accept responsibility for having ruined everything with Vedie. He's not coming home to me tonight, and I know the reason.

To put it in the barest of terms, it's because I'm a damned cold person.

I lack the emotional capacity to bond. I never let Vedie forget that my house isn't his house and is definitely not our home. That he's a guest in my life. And what we have together is temporary.

And even if what we have together goes on forever, in my mind it will always be labeled as impermanent. Vedie knows this. And he tried to fix me by loving me, but he has finally learned how devastating and foolish it is to love a block of ice.

This is clearly what I want us both to believe. I've had many chances to allow him into my life in a more emotionally intimate way, and I've slammed the door on each occasion.

And so I'm alone on the beach.

Solitary in my private escape, the way I've always wanted it.

After releasing a long, deep sigh, something tells me to get up and move. Since I'm here alone, I strip off my shorts and jog naked down to the shore. I want to keep going until I'm waist-deep in the warm water, but I don't. I stop when the waves hit my ankles, and I look out at the ocean. This view used to be the only sight of beauty I needed in my life to inspire me enough to keep going. But I've seen something more beautiful. *Someone* more beautiful.

By the time I finally dive into the ocean, I've made a decision. Nothing specific. But I resolve to make more significant changes in the way I've existed for so long.

Maybe it's time for living.

AFTER NIGHT FALLS, I struggle to fall asleep. And when I finally do, dreams of the way Daniel tortured me snatch my brain and hold on. Each time I wake up flat on my back, I turn onto my side in search of Vedie, but he isn't there to hold me. He's with Sheila, brightening *her* life.

I lie in my bed thinking I should be happy—relieved, even—and thankful to have the burden of this complicated woman/man off my hands, for the moment at least. But I'm simply empty. That's all.

I remember the decision I made before I dove into the ocean earlier today: *I'm going to make some major changes in my life.* With this thought in mind, at last I find enough peace to sleep.

Chapter Seventeen

MATT

Sitting at the kitchen table, sipping on Vedie's blueberry tea, and trying to keep my mind on business, passes the time. Before I know it, it's noon, so I stand up, stretch, feed the cats, and head to the refrigerator to find lunch. I pull out the last bowl of corn chowder Vedie cooked for dinner several nights ago. It only takes a minute to heat it up in the microwave, and when I sit back at the table, for a moment, it's as if he's here with me. Vedie, who made this chowder with such attention to detail, worrying it wouldn't have enough flavor since I asked him not to include the bacon the recipe called for. But Vedie worried for nothing—the corn chowder is delicious.

Vedie...the man I love so much.

And there it is.

Denying my love for Vedie will not make it less real.

With every bite, I remind myself it's time to make some very necessary changes in my life.

Changes that scare the living hell out of me.

I can slowly address each area in which I'm emotionally deficient. There's no rush, because nobody is more patient than Vedie—and God knows, the list is damned long—but somehow, I'm confident he'll wait for me.

He can help to fix what's broken inside me. In fact, he's already started.

Vedie told me he loves me, scars and all. It was the last thing he said to me before I watched him walk away.

After rinsing the bowl and spoon, I put my mind to business, with the intention of getting ahead of the game so I can focus the next few days exclusively on fixing things with him.

VEDIE

I'm starting to wish I never said yes to Sheila when she asked me to sleep at her house tonight. She offered me a place to go where I can think about what I want with Mateo—and if I want to stay with Mateo. But I want to go home.

I want to make shit right with Mateo.

I'll tell him how good it'd be if he loved me. And if he can't hear what I say, I'll prove it with my body—one man to another. I'll grab him and hold him tight and take him to heaven with me.

It'll be good—he'll feel so warm and so sweet and so mine—and he'll smile when I say I love him, and I'll know he feels the same. Even if his soul is too damaged to let his lips speak those three words out loud.

It's almost closing time.

After I clear all of the tables on the beach, I'm going to find Sheila and ask her if she'll drop me off at the cottage. And I'll tell her I'm not satisfied with sharing only deep friendship with Mateo, as I told her earlier tonight. Not when I can see in Mateo's eyes that he loves me...and I see his love every time he looks at me.

The beach is dark.

Somebody doused the two big tiki torches nearest to the shore, which isn't supposed to happen until the very end of the night. And I think there's still a customer sitting at table number fifteen, where it's darkest.

He doesn't say *"Hey, dude"* or *"Nice night, huh?"* or anything at all.

He just stares.

It hits me real sudden and hard. *This can't be good.*

As I step closer, I can see he's staring at me.

Staring through me. And I know...

"I figured this day would come, sooner or later." I'm shocked my voice doesn't tremble.

When he stands and grabs me, I drop my tub of dishes. He shakes me harder than I've ever gotten shook, only to throw me down on the beach after. All I can hope is Sheila doesn't come to the water's edge to find out why I dropped the dishes. *I'm* already dead as a doornail, but there's no need for her to get mixed up in this pain.

"Can't you see I'm ready for this? I've been ready..." I meant to speak with sureness, but my words come out as a scared whisper. Nervousness makes me lick my lips.

I start to stand, but an angry fist slams into my jaw, and my ass hits the sand again.

"You want me...and nobody else does...so I'm gonna come with you." I don't look at him again. I already know what I'll see in his eyes, and I really don't need that kind of mind-fuck right now. "You drove here?"

He nods. I have a damned strong feeling about what's waiting for me in the car.

And it's not good.

"I know how to get to the parking lot without going through the restaurant. Come this way..."

The least I can do for Sheila and Angie is make a clean escape. I've caused everybody around here enough problems already.

So I sneak off into the darkness, followed by my worst luck ever.

MATT

More than anything, I wanted to go to The Only Tiki Hut for dinner so I could watch Vedie as he bounced around the bar, delivering drink orders and filling his plastic tub with dirty dishes, smiling in my direction every chance he got. But instead, I focused on work, finishing as much as I could so when I pick him up, there'd be no distraction.

I don't have any specific plans for the soul-spilling conversation we'll have—detailing how I'll change for the better—because I don't yet know exactly how I'm going to modify my behavior. I don't actually have to explain to him where I went wrong and how I'm going to make it better. Maybe, instead, I can show him by being a better man, starting at ten o'clock tonight.

Feeling completely unlike the Matt I'm used to being— I'm this optimistic guy wearing a shit-eating grin—I pull into the parking lot of The Only Tiki Hut at a few minutes before ten. Vedie probably won't recognize me with this huge smile. I sit in my truck and watch as the few remaining customers leave the restaurant and head for their cars. I always keep an eye out for Joey, so I scan the parking lot, but there's no sign of the man. At ten fifteen, Sheila, still in her uniform, crosses the parking lot on the way to her car. I jump out of the truck and race over to say hello.

"Hey, Sheila."

I smile when she reaches out for a hug, but then she pushes me back, a strange look on her face. "What're you doing here, Matt? I thought Vedie was sick at home."

I drop my arms to my sides. "What are you talking about?"

She's confused. "Well, you know how Vedie was supposed to come to my house last night? When it was time for me to leave, he was already gone, but he texted me and said he had a killer headache, and so he was gonna go home with you. But, duh, you already know all this." She reaches up and pulls out the clip that's been holding her white-blonde hair on the top of her head. It spills onto her shoulders. "Then today, he texted Angie and said he had a stomach flu and wasn't gonna be able to work tonight."

"He did?" I feel instantly sick with dread but focus on making sense of what she just told me. "Uh, look Sheila..."

"Yeah? What's up?" She unlocks her car door.

"Vedie...he wasn't at home last night." We stare at each other in shock as we try to put the pieces together. "And he wasn't with me today."

She drops her keys to the sidewalk. "Then where the hell is he?"

"Shit. Sheila, I don't know." I blurt out my question. "You haven't seen Joey around here, have you?"

"No—he hasn't been around; I don't think." She squats and starts feeling around the ground for her keys but looks up at me suddenly. "Oh God, you don't think he's in danger, do you?"

I kneel down beside her on the pavement. "I'm sure he's fine. He has to be."

"Should we go to the police?"

"I don't know if he's been gone long enough...and besides, I...I upset him the other day. He may have left because of me, and he doesn't want to be found quite yet."

"What do you mean, you upset him?" We're no longer having a quiet conversation. She's yelling at me.

But I'm still here, in mind and body.

"I...it was...shit, Sheila, that's our business, but he might've wanted to get some space from me."

"Jesus, Matt, you better not have driven the kid off... But no matter what happened, we've gotta find him and make sure he's okay. And I don't think the police'll start looking for him until forty-eight hours has passed." She stops talking to take a deep breath. "Listen, I'll get Betsy, and the three of us can search him out. Have you tried calling him?"

"I had no reason to. I thought he was working."

Sheila pulls her cell phone from her apron and dials, and after a minute says, "The call went straight to voice mail."

I'm sure Vedie would answer Sheila's call if he could, even if he wouldn't answer mine. "Where do we start looking? I don't know anybody he knows besides you and..."

Sheila pulls herself up off the ground. "Did you ever even ask him who he knows?"

She's furious at me, and I accept it because she has a right to be. I'm angry at myself, too.

"I'm gonna go talk to Betsy about this. Meanwhile, why don't you go back to your place and make sure he's not there. Keep your phone with you. I'll be in touch."

THE DRIVE BACK to my cottage never seemed so long.

I run up the walkway and across the porch, and barge into the cottage, yelling, "Vedie! Are you here? Vedie!"

He doesn't reply, so I go into the bedroom and then the bathroom to make sure all his things are still here. I half expect them to be gone, just like Vedie. Vanished from my life—nothing but a memory. I've experienced complete and drastic changes in my life within the space of a single day before. I know the meaning of "here today, gone tomorrow" better than anybody. But his bin of clothes remains untouched in my bedroom, as do the cosmetics, lotions, and perfume bottles in the bathroom, and his bike on my porch. He hasn't returned to collect his belongings. Wherever he is, he didn't plan to stay there long.

As I dial Sheila, the cats swarm around my feet, as though they detect my agitation and are trying to comfort me.

And I am very agitated.

Alone. Destroyed. Guilty. Shocked. Terrified.

But I'm still here. I'm aware. I'm dealing with this.

Vedie means that much to me.

"VEDIE'S NOT HERE," I tell Betsy, who answers Sheila's cell phone. "Is he at your place?"

"No, he's not here either. But we have a few ideas of where to go and look."

"Tell me where."

Betsy puts the phone speaker on. Sheila asks, "Hey, Matt. You doing okay?"

Other than being impatient for more information, I'm fine. "Yeah. Tell me where I should go to look for Vedie."

"I personally think Joey has him," Betsy interjects, "but I guess we have to check out the other options so as to be sure."

If it's possible for blood to freeze, mine does. The thought of Joey having control over Vedie, after what he did to him on the beach, terrifies me.

"How about if Betsy and I go to his old apartment building and ask the guys who live there if they've seen him?

They always liked Vedie and were willing to lend a hand if he needed it."

"Okay, Sheila, but what about me—what should I do?" I need to do something. I can't sit here and worry.

Sheila doesn't hesitate. "I think you should go back to The Only Tiki Hut and get the dirt on Joey. His last name is Rundell, if I remember correctly. Find out where he lives, go there, and talk to his wife to see where he might be if he's not living with her."

"You think Angie will give me the info?"

"You won't know until you ask," Betsy replies.

She's right. "You think Angie will still be at work?"

"If you get your ass right back there. She's always the last person to leave, around midnight."

I'm already heading toward the door. "I'm on my way."

"HIS NAME IS Joseph Richard Rundell. He lives at 20987 Palmetto Trail, apartment 1A, in Tully. However, his wife, Vivian, drove here last week to pick up his final paycheck, as she said he's among the missing, and she's got bills to pay with his name on them."

I'm mildly surprised Angie is willing to give up confidential information about Joey, but he never gave her notice or even the common courtesy of a phone call to inform her he wasn't returning to work. Maybe she feels Joey owes her, and she's collecting by giving out the info I need. "Thank you, Angie."

"But you didn't get those facts from me." Her all-business attitude seems to be softened by a genuine concern for Vedie. "Vedie texted me to let me know he wasn't feeling well tonight, and I thought it was weird because I figured he'd have called. He's not scheduled to work for the next two days, so I guess I wouldn't have known he went missing until next week. But if you and Sheila say he's gone, I don't doubt you."

"I plan on finding him tonight."

"I hope you do. Let me know if there's anything more I can do."

"There is one more thing."

"Just name it."

"Do you remember what time he left last night? Did he say goodnight? And did he change his clothes? Was he acting strangely at all?" I blurt out all my questions.

Angie stands up behind the bar. "Slow down...one at a time. Let's see... The last I saw of him was at about nine thirty when he was wiping down the unoccupied bar stools in Sheila's section. I didn't notice whether he'd changed his clothes, but he never said good-bye. He was all of a sudden gone."

"Did he seem nervous?"

She turns the light out above the bar, and we're left in total darkness, with the exception of a single blue, flickering light. "Come to think of it, he did seem out of sorts, at least for the last part of the night."

"How so?"

"He seemed to have a lot on his mind. I don't remember the details—it was still busy—but he told me he was going to clean the barstools, and Vinny was going to clear off the rest of the tables. He wasn't his usual cheerful self, though."

This is more info than I'd hoped for. Vedie was scared and hiding from somebody—Joey, probably. Or maybe he was just depressed about how I didn't reciprocate his declarations of love. "Thanks, Angie. I'll let you know what I find out."

"Good luck."

As soon as I get to my truck, I call and relay the information to Sheila and Betsy.

I DRIVE OUT to Tully after midnight, although Sheila and Betsy think I should wait until the morning. They told me Joey's wife is probably alone there, and if I knock on the door in the middle of the night, I'll scare the shit out of her. My perspective is different: if Joey is holding Vedie, I'll hopefully see the man's old silver sedan or hear screaming or get some other type of clue he has him. And if he does, I can save him. It seems simple.

Even in the middle of the night, Palmetto Trail is pretty busy. It's a four-lane, two-direction road speckled with fast-food restaurants and strip malls, occasional low-budget hotels, and rundown housing units. It isn't difficult to find the correct address. I park my truck in the lot behind the tired, gray stucco building, sheltered on all sides by gangly shrubbery. After surveying the lot for Joey's sedan and not finding it, I walk around the building. Apartment 1A is on the bottom floor, so I skulk into the building's shadows and take a look inside each of the windows. Although the shades are drawn, the material is relatively sheer, and I can see into the house.

I check out the living room and see only worn furniture and a tattered rug. No Vedie, no Joey. I'm also able to look into the bedrooms. In one, a little boy is sleeping with a cat at the foot of the bed, and in the other, Joey's wife Vivian is out like a light.

Satisfied that Vedie isn't duct taped to a kitchen table in this apartment, I head back to the truck and get as comfortable as I can. I plan to knock on the apartment door first thing in the morning.

I don't expect to get any rest at all, but I manage to slip in and out of sleep for the next few hours. And when day breaks, I wake up with a start. As soon as I collect myself, I return to the apartment building and knock on the door.

A dark-haired woman opens it and says bluntly, "I don't want any. Especially if you're trying to push God on me."

It's hard to believe I could possibly look respectable enough to be mistaken for a salesperson of any kind after having spent the night in my truck. I smooth down the front of my shirt. "I'm not selling anything, ma'am. I'm looking for Joe Rundell. Have you seen him lately?"

"Have I seen him? The bastard left me and his kid high and dry. I gotta pay rent on this place, and I got no car no more, and alls I got is my job at the Lowe's downtown to make ends meet. Rotten rat-bastard!" Vivian Rundell doesn't invite me in for coffee, but neither does she demand that I get lost. She's in her bathrobe, brushing out her wet, tangled hair, and squinting with disgust. Mrs. Rundell doesn't much care for the subject of our conversation.

"Do you know where he's staying right now?"

"The only people who'd take him in are his druggy cousins who live in Leighton. It's a fucking crack house; they'll take in any loser there."

"You don't happen to have their address, do you?"

"I don't send them no Christmas cards, if that's what you're asking. But if you go to Leighton and find the gas station on the corner of North and Davison...well, they run that shit hole. Probably launder money outta there, if you ask me, and they live in the building behind it. You can't miss the eyesore. I think it was red at one point, but most of the paint's seen better days."

"Thanks, Mrs. Rundell, you've been very helpful."

"If you see the rat-bastard, tell him Vivian said to eat shit and die, 'kay?"

SHEILA AND I sit next to each other on the loveseat in their living room. "So I guess I'm going to head to Leighton today, and hopefully, I'll find Vedie."

She wrinkles her nose. "Have you ever been to Leighton? Some parts aren't safe. I hope Vedie isn't there."

Betsy comes into the room with a tray of sandwiches. "You aren't going over there alone, Crazy Matt. I'll come along for the ride."

"I'll be okay on my own." I was okay on my own for the past ten years, until Vedie came and gave me a life, and with it, countless reasons to care.

"Not happening. So chow down on a couple of these babies, and we'll be off." She sticks the plate of sandwiches in my face.

I grab a couple PBJs and a bottle of water from the coffee table. I'm in a hurry. Time not spent searching for Vedie is time when my imagination runs wild. All I can see when I blink is Vedie in my place as a seven-year-old captive—duct taped to the legs of a kitchen table, inhaling the scent of fried bacon and waiting for his rapist to enter the room. "I think we should get going right now."

Sheila grabs a sandwich but stops before taking a bite. "What happened with you that upset Vedie the other day? I could tell something was bothering him at work, but he said he didn't want to get into the details."

I want to run and hide, and if I can't do that, to mentally cut and run. Instead, I answer the question. "Vedie told me how he felt about me the night before, and I...I didn't say...the same words in return."

Sheila nods, as does Betsy.

"He said he loved you, and you just stared at him with the same guilty eyes you're looking at me with right now?" Betsy doesn't cut me any slack.

"That's about how it went down." I have to look away—I feel like shit. I don't deserve any slack.

"Well, you should know this—Vedie wasn't planning to leave you any time soon, Matt."

Sheila's eyes fill as she speaks, and I'm not sure if I want to hear what she's about to tell me. But since today I'm facing the music, I look directly at her and listen.

"Vedie told me he was going to accept you exactly as you are—a man who is unsure of relationships, unable to make a commitment, and stuck in the middle of being a man and a boy. He wasn't about to pressure you to be someone you're not, because you never expected him to be anything other than Vedie."

These words strike me hard. Vedie saw the truth of our situation together, and of us as individuals, far better than I did.

I shove the rest of a sandwich in my mouth and stand up. "I'm off to Leighton."

"I'm coming." Betsy grabs another couple of sandwiches.

"Me too." Sheila stands up. "Let's go find Vedie."

BETSY DRIVES HER Jeep Wrangler because we're hopeful. Three of us are going to look for him, and if we find him, there will be four—too many to squeeze comfortably into my truck.

"The gas station is coming up on the corner, on the left." I point across the street to the dilapidated building with a couple of fuel pumps out front.

"The corner of North and Davison, right?"

"Yeah," I reply as we drive right by. "We passed it, Betsy!"

"Well, I'm not getting gas, dude." She turns the Jeep around, drives back toward the gas station, and pulls into an open parking space on the street.

"We're gonna walk over and try to check out the house behind the station without anybody seeing us."

"Oh, right." I'm not thinking straight. We can't very well pull right up to the pumps and ask the attendant if Vedie's there. "They might notice three of us walking around their property, don't you think?"

"Definitely." Betsy looks at Sheila. "Sheila, I think you should wait here in the driver's seat."

"You want me to be ready to go in case you find him and we have to take off fast?" she asks, and Betsy nods.

"It's a long shot, you know. He's probably not even here." I have to bring myself and them back down to earth. We're on a fool's errand, and it's best to be prepared for failure.

"Well, it's worth a shot, right?" Betsy stays hopeful, which is what I need.

I get out of the back of the Jeep without answering. We all know what needs to be done.

Sheila climbs into the driver's seat, and we look at each other for a silent second before Betsy and I head toward the house, walking slowly, as we have no real plan in place.

"What a dump," Betsy says, looking at the monstrous red building behind the gas station.

"How about if we cut through the neighbor's side yard? If we stay by the shrubs, we won't be as easy to see." It's not much of a plan, but it's all I can come up with.

"Sounds as good as any other idea."

I look around to see if anyone is watching us, and other than cars passing by and a few people at the gas station, no one is in eyeshot.

We make our way through the grass to the old red house and circle it, staying close to the building. I look into each window as I pass and see nothing but a huge mess in the rooms. No one seems to be home. We linger beside the front porch, listening for anything out of the ordinary, but hear nothing except the sounds of traffic.

"Maybe we should look on the nearby streets to see if Joey's car is parked anywhere around here." My ideas aren't creative, but I'm trying.

"Why don't I go to the door and knock, and if someone answers, ask a couple of questions before we leave?"

It's true that an unannounced woman at the door might seem less intimidating than a hulking man. "What will you say?"

"I'll just say we're looking for Vedie Wilson."

I'm not sure if this is a good or bad idea, but I'm no Sherlock Holmes. "I guess it can't hurt."

Betsy heads for the front doorsteps, runs up, and knocks on the door. To my amazement, Joey answers. I can't stop myself from sprinting up the stairs to join them.

"You...you're from the bar—you're Vedie's pissed-off friend!" He points at me. "What you want, huh?"

"I want to know where Vedie is." I'd planned to stay in control, but this man tried to strangle and drown Vedie on the beach and left him there for dead. "I know you have him!"

Betsy comes to my side and wraps her arm around my shoulders. I realize she's trying to calm me down, an impossible task.

"I don't have that little bitch! What would I want with her or him or whatever the fuck it is?" Joey clearly wasn't expecting company. He's wearing a once-white T-shirt that's ripped at the neck, a pair of grease-stained tan shorts he didn't bother to button, and a gold chain. He steps back into the kitchen. "Come in and check—I don't have that friggin' loser!"

I barge past him and march right into the kitchen. "Vedie! Vedie, are you in here?"

Betsy's at my heels until she heads up the stairs to check the bedrooms. "Hey, Vedie, yell loud if you're here!" she calls from above.

I scramble around the kitchen and then go to what I think is a living room, but it's hard to say because the decor is comprised of a mass of empty pizza boxes, tables cluttered with dirty bongs, liquor and beer bottles, other random trash, and an occasional metal chair.

But no Vedie.

Betsy comes into the living room. "He's not in the upstairs bedrooms or bathroom."

I rush back to the kitchen and grab Joey by the neck of his T-shirt. "Where the fuck is he?"

He struggles, but I don't let go.

"Tell me where the fuck he is!"

"Probably out fuckin' some other clueless dude, but the little bitch isn't here—I don't have him!"

I pull back with the fist that's not grasping his shirt and punch him hard in the jaw. "You tried to kill him that night."

"Asshole, let's get one thing straight." He rubs his jaw, and then he makes a fist of his own, but wisely doesn't throw a punch. "If I meant to kill Vedie Wilson, he'd be dead right now. So leave me the fuck alone!" Joey is a poor excuse for a human being, but I somehow know he doesn't have Vedie.

I push him against the wall and finally let go of his T-shirt. "You fit just fine right here in this cockroach-infested dump! If I ever see you on the island again, consider yourself worse off than how I found Vedie on the beach the night you made the biggest mistake of your worthless life!"

To my satisfaction, Joey looks nervous. With his hand again on his jaw, he gulps once and grumbles, "Get the fuck outta my house."

I glance down at the loser one more time and somehow hold back the urge to kick his ass while screaming that his wife wants him to eat shit and die.

"Come on, Matt," Betsy says. "This waste-of-breath doesn't have Vedie."

Chapter Eighteen

MATT

There wasn't any more we could do, so after we left Joey's house, we went to the police station and filed a missing person report. The cops took the information and dutifully assured us they'd look into it but reminded us patiently that Vedie is an adult and has the right to go missing if he so chooses. I got the feeling they think he's something of an adult runaway, who, after living several months on the island of misfit toys, decided to blow away in the breeze and start over somewhere else. They think he's a homeless person, of sorts. He has no legal address and no family to speak of, and a job as a busboy, from which he seems to come and go.

They could be right, who knows? Not me, because I chose not to ask Vedie any pertinent questions—I refused to learn about his life experiences and background. I figured it would hurt less to lose a stranger than a person I knew, understood, and empathized with when he inevitably left me. And for all I know, the police are right. Maybe Vedie realized that since the flower of romantic love wasn't blooming here on Placida Island, he should move on to take his chances on growing a garden elsewhere.

I pull into the driveway and sit in my truck for a few minutes, mentally reviewing Vedie's attempts to know and understand me—attempts that were in no way mutual. And

I can't rid my mind of the possibility that he could now be in the same situation I was in as a child—abducted, restrained, and unable to get away. With this idea as motivation, I leave the truck and head up the path to the cottage. A cottage empty of souls, with the exception of the four cats that must be pretty damn hungry by now. I enter the kitchen to a chorus of meows and immediately fill the food and water bowls with a few soft words of apology for being late with their supper.

After feeding the cats, I head into the living room. Vedie has created a lively personality in the formerly bland room, with the bright rainbow curtain across the window and the stretchy-lace-top picture hanging over the couch, and as I look around more, I notice tiny details I'd missed until now. Dried flowers and beach grass tied with a ribbon hanging on the bathroom door, and rocks from the beach, painted with silly faces, scattered on the coffee table. And there's a flower-shaped velvet pillow, cut from a length of stretchy rainbow cheetah-print fabric we bought at Landon's Craft Shop, hand sewn with black thread from my tiny sewing kit, carefully placed in the very center of the couch. Vedie was slowly, but surely, making this cottage into a home.

I'm not certain whose home, though, because I never fully welcomed him here.

I drop onto the couch, place my head in my hands, and try to make myself wish I'd never met him. But it's impossible. Vedie's love turned me into a person again by bringing everything dead inside me back to life. He saw my scars—those on my heart and on my back—as beautiful and unique, important parts of me. And even though I'm stunned by the loss of him, feeling hurt and desperate might be a step above being a hollow shell of a human being.

The jury is still out on this.

Stretching my tired body across the couch, I rack my brain for a plan. I can't let this be the end of us. If even an outside chance exists that he was taken against his will, I need to do everything I can to find and release him. I can't let him suffer the way I did.

No one deserves that.

Where is he? And wherever he is, does he want to be found?

If I find him, do I want to bring him back to this cottage and keep him here as a permanent part of my life?

Do I really love him?

Once my lips stop moving with the frenzy of questions, they curve into a smile because my heart knows all of the answers.

I close my eyes and wait for sleep to come.

I AWAKEN TO the ring of my cell phone. I grab it. "Vedie?"

"No, Matt. It's just me." Sheila. My heart sinks.

"Any word from Vedie?" I already know the answer. If there were news, she'd have led with it.

"No, sorry. But Betsy and I were talking, and we remembered something Vedie told us when we first met him. I think it might have something to do with why he's missing."

Suddenly, I'm wide-awake. "What is it?"

"He told us he was in hiding from his family and a few friends who live in Boston. He was always saying he was worried they'd find him."

"He mentioned that to me, too."

"People from home could have found him and dragged him back to Boston."

Why hadn't I thought of that? I hit my head with a flattened palm. "How could they have found him?"

"Last week, Vedie told me when he got paid, he was going to mail some money back home to his mother. We got paid a couple days later, and his family could have figured out where he's hiding from the letter he wrote or the postage stamp on the envelope."

"I guess it's possible." I try to contain my nervous excitement, but my voice still trembles. "I think we're onto something."

"If they're still here in Florida, they could be in one of the local motels." I must be on speakerphone because now Betsy's chiming in.

"We should drive around and check the nearby motels for cars with Massachusetts plates," I'm thinking out loud. "We might come across them...unless they flew here and rented a car, or they've already headed north."

"It's still worth driving around and checking, though," Sheila says. "We can pick you up in less than an hour. Then we'll go to every single motel in the area."

"Thanks, you guys."

My hope is renewed.

"MANNY'S SLEEP AND Stay is the only hotel on the island we haven't checked, so our next stop will have to be in Windward." Betsy's voice has lost its excitement. We've already been to four motels and found nothing to indicate Vedie's been there.

"After we look around here, I'll take you guys for a quick lunch, then we can search the hotels and motels over the bridge."

Betsy pulls her Jeep into the motel parking lot, and we all hop out. There are only a few cars, but in the corner of the parking lot, there's a Chrysler sedan with Mass plates. Without any real expectations, I walk over to it and peer into the driver's window.

And there it is.

A leopard-print backpack on the floor of the passenger seat.

It takes everything in me not to scream. I scramble toward Sheila and Betsy who are busy looking at the other cars in the lot.

"What is it, Matt?" Sheila senses my urgency. "Tell us!"

"His backpack... Vedie's backpack is in that Chrysler in the corner of the lot! Mass plates, too!"

"Oh, my God!" Sheila rushes toward the car, but I chase her down and grab her arm to stop her. "We don't know what room they're in. We've got to find out and then get inside before they realize we're here."

Sheila's eyes are filled with tears, and she's now anxiously gasping for breath, as am I. Betsy's the only one of us who is somewhat in control. "I'll go to the office and tell them I have a pizza delivery for some young men under the name of Wilson."

"Good idea." I take hold of Sheila and pull her back to the Jeep. "Come on and get in the driver's seat and wait for us. Remember, we might need to pull out of this place in a hurry and you have to be ready to drive."

She nods and gets into the Jeep.

Betsy comes out of the office. "The Wilson party is in room twelve."

I cannot believe we've found him so quickly; it was so much easier than I anticipated. "Should we knock and when they open the door barge in?"

"I think it's our best bet, Matt."

As Betsy and I are throwing together our very rough plan, the door to room twelve opens and three men come out. One of them so closely resembles Vedie he could be his twin, but because of the way he carries himself—confident to the point of arrogance—I can tell, even from across the parking lot, it's not Vedie. The men pile into the sedan and drive away.

"If he's in there, he could be alone now," I say.

Betsy nods. "Well, we should get over there. I'll tell Sheila to pull the Jeep up to room twelve."

"How are we going to get in?" I'm usually fairly clever, but right now, my nerves are shot and I'm useless.

"Why don't you go around back and see if there's a sliding door or a window? If you can't get in that way, we'll have to knock. Or bribe the maid."

I'm already moving as I call back to Betsy, "I'll head around back and see if I can get in!"

The back side of the motel is dismal, decorated with piles of household trash, stacked wood, and other debris. Unit twelve is the third from the end, and as soon as I identify it, I rush to the back window and press my face against the screen.

There, on a chair in the middle of the room, bound and beaten, is Vedie.

I glance around to see if anyone else is with him.

Unless someone's in the bathroom, he seems to be alone.

Common sense tells me to run to the office and let the manager know what's happening so he can unlock the room and call the police, but Vedie looks so scared and hurt I can't wait.

I pick up a cement block from the ground and slam it through the window. "Vedie! I'm here—I'm gonna take you home!"

At the sound of the glass breaking, Vedie's head, hanging down on his chest, lifts suddenly and then drops again. I think he's aware I'm here. I kick out the rest of the window, climb through, step onto the bed, and practically leap through the air to get to him.

Placing my fingers on his chin, I lift his face off of his chest and see evidence of a brutal beating. Swollen lips and eyes, a cut on his cheek...and his nose may never be the same. I'm filled with rage but simultaneously aware of the pressing need to get him out of here. Seeing that his hands are duct taped together and his ankles are taped to the legs of the chair, I grit my teeth and swallow hard to deal with my instinctive feelings of helplessness.

Memories of being taped to Daniel's kitchen table rise up to haunt me, but I manage to fight my fear and look around, searching for tools to free him. I see a small knife on the bedside table in the midst of a dozen empty beer cans, grab it, and cut through the bindings.

"Vedie...hey, are you with me?" I take his face in my hand and shake it very gently.

"Teo...I wanna go home." His voice is raspy and trembling, and his eyes don't open because they're too swollen, but he seems to be aware.

"And I'm taking you there, Vedie. I'm taking you home." And when I say home, I mean *our* home. Not just *my cottage*, with Vedie in residence as a houseguest. I scoop him into my arms, cross the room, and open the door with one hand. Betsy rushes to my side and helps me carry him to the back seat of the Jeep.

"To the hospital?" Sheila asks shakily.

"No!" Vedie is suddenly more alert, though his eyes remain swollen shut. "I'm gonna be fine...and I wanna go home. Please take me home."

"Shelia, can you drive us to our cottage? Vedie wants to go home."

MATT'S JOURNAL DATED JULY 2015

Sometimes, I think about how it was when I finally got home. The first thing that pops into my mind is how things weren't the way I'd always dreamed they'd be on all those long afternoons when I was pinned beneath Daniel in his lumpy bed at the back of the trailer.

In my imagination, the Matthew of that point in time—a shaggy-haired, tattooed, pierced, teenage smoker—would return home to live it up in the fine home I barely remembered, with a mother who doted on him, a father who lived for nothing more than to teach him to drive the BMW, and two older brothers who waited in line to toss around a football with him between beers. *Ha!*

The reality of the situation was the house had rules, the mother had expectations, the father could barely look at him, and the two brothers had moved on to college and law school and new lives.

None of us knew how we fit together in the North household. And the media was fucking relentless, so much so my mother attempted to grant them a "televised family interview" to get them off our backs, but I ultimately refused to participate.

Everything was the opposite of how I'd imagined it. Our family needed to start from scratch to rebuild our bond, and sadly, our best efforts to do this didn't work. In other words, the whole thing was a fucking disaster.

I needed time and space, and what I got was constant questioning and smothering.

I needed to build up trust in my parents; instead, they judged me. I wasn't the same as before. I didn't look the same, think the same, or feel the same. Nobody understood they couldn't simply turn back the clock of life so everything could go back to how it used to be— how it was *supposed* to be. And I knew I wouldn't be able to explain my feelings to them, so I gave up before I tried. Besides, some of what happened to me was so ugly I didn't want them to know about it. Not only was I embarrassed, I needed to protect them from that kind of evil.

These feelings of incompatibility with the world were at the root of more than a decade of self-imposed isolation.

So, on the ten-year anniversary of my move to Placida Island, am I lonely?

Well, I'm not being questioned and stared at and pried open, which are positives. But after ten years on an island, rarely exchanging so much as a "hello" with other human beings—yeah, I'm lonely.

But this is also my destiny. I have no clue how to change direction.

Chapter Nineteen

MATT

With my help, Vedie is able to walk into the cottage on his own two feet, which reassures me to some extent that he's not permanently injured. I want so badly to ask what happened in the motel room and if he needs to see a doctor and when can we call the police, but all he wants is to clean up in the bathroom.

Sheila rushes to the kitchen to get him a bottle of water and a bag of ice—although I fear it's too late for ice to do any good—and Betsy heads to the living room to worry. But I'm not about to leave his side. In the bathroom, I help him remove his work uniform and fill the tub with warm water. I can see most of the damage was done to his face; I don't think they stripped him down to beat him because the scratches and scrapes to his arms and legs stop where his T-shirt and shorts begin. But his face is a mess, and I'm concerned about possible head injury.

As Vedie bathes, I offer him the bottle of water Sheila fetched, and then clean all the injuries to his face with the softest washcloth I can find. Finally, I rinse the dried blood from his dreads.

"Sorry," he mumbles.

"You have nothing to be sorry for."

"Did I have you worried?"

"Maybe slightly," I lie.

And then, for the first time since I was eight years old, I let myself cry—not in loud sobs, but in silent tears streaming from my eyes, which I make no effort to restrain.

Struggling with a tight throat, I manage to confess, "More than slightly worried—much more."

Vedie manages to lift his puffy eyelids enough to look at me. "Then I'm sorry." His voice is raspy, probably from screaming, and I wonder why no one at the motel heard his cries and called the police.

"No, Vedie."

His eyes close again, and I know he needs rest. With a big bath towel in my arms, I scoop him from the tub and dry him carefully.

"So thirsty, Teo." He holds up the already-empty water bottle.

"I'll put you to bed and bring you some more water and a mug of blueberry tea."

When he smiles, his lip splits and a drop of blood rolls down his chin.

SHEILA AND BETSY are waiting in the living room. "Thank you...thanks for helping me." My voice is almost as weak as Vedie's was, but I know they understand the depth of my appreciation.

"We all love Vedie," is Sheila's simple answer. Betsy nods in agreement.

"Yes, we all do." And I do. I love the man curled in a fetal ball in my bed.

The realization that I almost lost the only person in the world I love is crushing, but strangely, I never once lost my awareness as I struggled to find him. I somehow rose to the challenge of locating the man I cannot live without, the one who makes my house a home and, with four cats, my family. "I'll take care of him, and when he tells me about what happened, and we decide what we're going to do about it, I'll call you."

I hug my friends—I almost cling to them—out of sheer thankfulness. But it's more than that. I hold them close because of my strong feelings for them. I think I might love these women, too.

As soon as they head out the door, I rush to the bedroom where Vedie's curled up on his side, his eyes closed more peacefully than before, and slip beneath the sheets behind him. I press my body against his back, and he pushes on me. I can't help but cry a little bit more when I take him into my arms and kiss his damp hair.

He pushes his back even harder against my chest, and I swear, this close to him, I smell his fear over the scent of the soap on his skin. Though worn out, I somehow still feel strong and can't stop my arms from pulling him against me.

I only have to wait a minute or two before we are both lost to this world.

I'M FUCKING SHOCKED.

When I wake up, Vedie isn't in my arms where he fell asleep.

Where I need him to be.

Where I want him to be.

Instead, he's standing in the corner of the room by his bin of clothing, pulling out each item and folding it into its smallest form before replacing it.

"What are you doing?"

His features are all swollen, but his eyes have clearly shifted in my direction, and he's staring at me with a blank, almost battle-weary hollowness. "I'm packing."

"Why?" I sit up quickly. "Why are you packing your things, Vedie?" A chill of fear and dread shoots to the tips of each of my fingers. "There's no reason for you to pack."

"They know where I am now. I can't stay here. Not safe." He sways a bit, and I fear he'll fall. I leap out of bed, and my hands come down on his sides to hold him steady. I have no intention of letting him stumble and fall ever again.

"We'll call the police and report them, and they'll go to jail for what they did to you. And then you'll be safe."

He shakes his head. "No can do. Mama would never forgive me." He places his neatly folded rainbow minidress in the bin and turns to face me. "Can I stay until tomorrow, Mateo? I'm in no shape to travel just yet."

I stare at him, stunned. I can barely grasp what's happening right before my eyes. The man I love, whose face is literally destroyed, with still-raw defensive wounds covering his fingers and hands, and doing his best to see me through an unfocused gaze, is standing at the end of my bed packing his belongings so he can leave before he inconveniences me. "Vedie, you aren't going anywhere."

"But I am, Mateo. I'm halfway gone already."

I must look at him with a question in my eyes because he readily explains.

"My head told my heart that it's time to go."

I worried he would stumble and fall, but I'm the one to hit my knees on the bedroom floor. "No."

"I'm nothing but trouble," He lightly runs one finger along the slice under his left eye. "Mama always said, 'Boy, you're nothing but a handful of problems wrapped up in way too much drama and a flowery sundress,' and the woman was right." He smiles as he reminisces about his mother's perpetual rejection, which I find intolerable.

"She was wrong." I'm a quiet guy, and I'm not exactly sure that, in my case, still waters run deep. There has never been too much I've felt needed to be said in life, but I'm going to try my best to express my feelings to Vedie because he's worth it. And *we're* worth it. "It's the world that's full of problems and prejudices and fear and hate, Vedie. Not you."

He drops to his knees beside me. "I brought trouble and worry and pain down on you, didn't I?"

"You made me feel. My heart was a fucking block of ice—and you melted it."

He looks confused. "But I'm not a smart and pretty young lady you can bring home to your mama."

"You *are* smart and pretty." I don't want a woman. I want Vedie, exactly as he is.

"I'm not even a proper gay dude. I'm like the mystery prize at the bottom of the Cracker Jacks box. You don't know what you gonna get, but you know it's not gonna be worth anything."

I place my hands on his shoulders, and he does his best to look into my eyes. "No, Vedie. You're special—you change with your moods, just as I do. I'm a man who can usually take care of himself, and to my surprise, sometimes I take pretty good care of you, but at other times I'm a boy who's lost, who separates from the here and now. And when I do, I need a gentle hand. I need you to help me find my way back. You hold me together. Every time I fall down and break, you fix me again."

He shakes his head.

"When you look at me, you see more than my scars. But even when you look at them, you don't cringe. You accept them. You understand how much endurance it took for me to survive what I went through to get them. And then you reach out and touch my scars with your gentle hand." This is the most I've ever said to one person at one time in my entire life.

"I was lucky as hell I got to be your gentle hand for a while, but the guys from home, they know where I work. They'll be back to beat the rest of the softness out of me—I can promise you that. And I can't go through it again. Nobody might be around to save me next time."

"But you don't work at the Tiki Hut anymore." Vedie's skeptical expression tells me he thinks I've totally lost it. "You work here now."

"Here?" A tiny drop of blood slides from his lower lip, and I wipe it away with the inside of my wrist.

I've done a lot of thinking in the past couple of days. It's time to share my thoughts, and I find myself eager. "I figured you could open an online craft shop right here from our home. And I can make you a website to help you sell your creations. I'm good at that part."

Vedie places his battered head into his torn-up hands. He speaks softly. "Why, Teo? Why are you doing all this shit for me?"

"Because."

He's impatient. His head is tilted, and he's holding his hands up. "Well, go on and spill it, then. And I don't have all day here."

He makes me smile even when he's trying to be bossy. "It's because I love you, and I don't want to you to leave. And if you leave, well, then I'd better start packing, too, because I'm going with you."

He sways to the right, and his swollen lids close over his patchy red eyes.

But I steady him as he kneels here, and then I help him up and to the bed. "Come on, let's lie down together. You shouldn't be on your feet doing this yet. You could have a head injury, and you need to tell me what happened and—"

"One thing at a time, Teo. And the one thing I wanna think about is that you love me. It's what you just said, ain't it?"

"I love you so much."

"I'm tired and my head hurts, and I haven't had a bite to eat in days...but first I've got to sleep some more...so I'm gonna fall asleep thinking about how you love me." He glances up at the fun-on-the-beach mobile hanging over our bed and smiles.

"Then we'll sleep more." I'm not leaving him alone.

We take our places in the bed, and this time, when we face each other and he wraps his arms around me, I hear a hum of happiness.

How he can be so happy—beaten until he's unrecognizable and probably forever scarred, hungry, and afraid—I'll never know. But this is Vedie.

And I think he might be mine.

Chapter Twenty

VEDIE

The time I spent in that motel room with Tyson, Marcus, and Juan was hell. And I'm changed from it. So, I guess they got what they wanted because I'm not sure if the softer side of me is ever going to show herself again. They battered and tortured her right out of me. The thing is, I don't know if no-more-soft-and-feminine Vedie is a deal-breaker for Mateo.

At first, I thought Mateo wanted me because I was a gay dude, and soon after that, I figured he liked me as mostly girly. It took a while for me to figure out he likes both parts of me.

But now, I haven't felt those soft, sweet, warm feelings that let my feminine side come out since the night I told Mateo I loved him and his mind went zooming out of his body, fast as cars speeding down 93 South on Friday afternoons in the summer on their way to Cape Cod. And then everybody I ran from in Boston came to Florida, found me in my hiding spot, and taught me that a dude can run, but he can't hide forever.

It's just that I've got to feel safe to be all of me—a man who's okay with showing the world his "feminine" side. And I don't feel safe anymore, not in my heart or my head. So a big and important part of me got scared off, just the way my brothers wanted.

I'm lying on my belly on the big brown beach towel, letting the afternoon sun sink into my skin while I embroider a tiny rainbow in the towel's corner with some special needles and thread from Landon's Craft Shop that Sheila and Betsy brought me yesterday. I can't concentrate as much as I want to because I keep on looking around to see if my brothers are coming out of the woods to grab me.

"I've been reading, Vedie." As it turns out, Mateo, who came quietly down from the cottage, is the one who shocks me, so I end up sticking my finger with the embroidery needle. "I've been reading online articles about trans people."

I've been home for four days, and my face is healing. I can see much better now that my eyelids aren't so swollen, and I've got some faith my nose is going to go back to its regular shape, for the most part. But I still can't bite into an apple without my stupid lip splitting. Mateo hasn't asked me any questions about what went down in the motel room. Or about where the girlish Vedie went. And now he's gone and done his homework about people like me. Go figure.

"What did you find out?" I'm not too sure I'm into being my new boyfriend's research project.

"I learned how many LGBTQ folks—especially nonbinary people who express their gender in ways that make others uncomfortable—live with way too much violence." Mateo drops down onto the sand beside me. "To be honest, what I read pissed me off."

I rub my aching chin. "It's not exactly news to me. It's kind of the story of my life."

"It's not right, Vedie."

"Maybe it's not right, but still, I tried to fit in so I could live in peace, you know? But I can't fit in, because even though I know I'm a man, I like to dress and act like a woman sometimes. So I either have to stop acting like the real me or live with fear." I weave my yellow-threaded needle into the edge of the towel, flip over, and stare up into Mateo's eyes that look as if they're made out of spun gold on this sunny day. "It's not a huge deal."

"You don't have to live with fear."

"Uh...yeah, I do." Mateo's looking at me like I'm America's Next Top Model, but I know my face is a wreck. And I've got no clue why he thinks there's a way out of all the pain and fear for somebody like me. Because there isn't.

"No. We can fight back."

I study his face for a few more seconds, trying to figure him out. "You're no fighter, Teo. Your head runs to hide whenever the going gets too tough."

His eyes tear up around the edges.

"But I can be strong for you, Vedie. And I'm getting stronger *because* of you."

I want to touch him because he's sweet, so I lift my battered hand and press it onto the smooth tanned skin of his arm. And I sigh because the way he's looking at me melts my heart.

"Tell me what happened with the guys from Boston."

I come right back with a line I'm pretty sure will stop him from asking me any more questions. "You gonna tell me about what went down with Daniel?"

Mateo's eyes slide off to the side, but they don't roll back. He's only thinking, not leaving me here alone on the beach. Finally he nods. "Yeah, I am."

I can't believe my ears. And I want to know so bad what scarred Mateo's body and soul when he was only a boy and turned him into the broken man who's sitting in front of me right now; I'm going to give him what he wants. I sit up so we can look at each other better. "Okay, then. I'll talk. I'll tell you what happened in the motel room."

"And when you're finished it'll be my turn to tell you about Daniel and me."

Mateo's scared shitless, but he covers my banged-up hand with his.

"I let them take me, Teo. My oldest brother Tyson—they sent him into the restaurant because he's the biggest dude in our family—was waiting for me down by the beach when I was clearing tables at the end of the night. When I saw him, I just gave up hope. I knew I got found out—and that my escape on this island was over." I don't mention how the beating started right there on the beach. "Didn't want to make a big scene at work, so at the end of my shift, I told Tyson I'd go with him. I snuck into the bathroom by the volleyball courts to grab my backpack, and then we went to where they were parked. My other brother, Marcus, and their friend Juan were waiting on us there in the car. I just got in, and we drove off."

"I would have helped you." Mateo's eyes look honest—he means what he's saying—and I believe him.

"Far as I knew then, you didn't love me. I wasn't gonna bring those assholes into your life if all we had was friendship."

"Friends help each other."

"Lovers sacrifice for each other, or so I heard."

"Fair enough." He takes my hand off its place on his arm and holds it tight, as if this will help me get through the rest of what I've got to say. "So, what happened next?"

I seriously don't want to talk about it. I lived out the very hell I feared since I left Boston and telling him the details is going to bring it all back. It'll be almost like living that hell all over again. But if I talk, he said he'd talk too. "They took me straight to the motel from The Only Tiki Hut. They'd already checked in. The room was all ready and waiting for me." My voice makes this weird cracking sound two times when I say, "ready and waiting." Guess I'm still scared shitless.

"How was it ready for you?" His expression tells me he's scared too, and maybe he doesn't really want to know the answer. But since he asked, I'm going to tell.

"They'd already stuck the chair you found me on in the middle of the room. A roll of duct tape was sitting on it, and a belt was coiled up on the bed, looking scary as hell. The three of them fought me all at the same time, because it's their way of having fun, and when they were done, they taped me to the chair." Mateo shivers when I tell him this part, as if it hits too close to home. "Plus, they had some of their other favorite tools."

"Like what?"

"They used to use paper clips on my..." My voice cracks again and I think, *I can't do this. I can't tell him of how my brothers and my friend, in trying to shame me out of being girly, clamped paper clips onto my nipples and left them there while I screamed.* "They didn't end up using them on me this time but seeing them reminded me they could."

"I get the picture."

Can eyes get darker? Because I think Mateo's just did.

"And they friggin' hate the way my voice sounds—they say I sound like a girl." I don't want to tell him this part, either, but I'm not going to chicken out now. "They stick the belt around my neck and pull tight, so I can't breathe. They let me breathe only if I show them that I can talk in a more manly way. It's like training a dog—they do it to me over and over, until I get it right."

Mateo trembles as if we're sitting on a snow bank, not on warm beach sand, but he stays quiet. I guess he hasn't got the right words to make me feel better, so he says nothing. Smart dude. But he lifts a shaky finger and touches the red mark on my neck that doesn't seem to want to fade away.

"Worst part is how they teach me it's not proper for a dude to suck another dude's dick."

Mateo's eyes go wide, and I know he's afraid to hear the details. Nonetheless, he says, "Tell me." *His* voice cracks this time.

"Ty says if I like things in my mouth so much..." I hold up a fist, and then I point to my mouth. "They're not small dudes, and they've got big hands. Can't get them all the way in, but it hurts my jaws real bad when they try."

"They try to stuff their fists in your mouth..." His voice trails away to nothing as he gets the picture. "Did they beat you more?"

"Well, of course they beat on me more—they're pissed off that I'm different from them. Except for Juan, but I'm the only one who knows how he acts when we're alone."

All of a sudden, I find myself captured in Mateo's arms, being hugged harder than I've ever got hugged before. It shocks me, even though at the same time, I'm into it. He takes this big gulping, raspy breath and says, "I want to kill them. I want to find them and kill them."

When he pushes me back so he can see my face again, I say, "That wouldn't do us any good. You'd end up in the slammer forever for committing triple murder."

"I still want to take them out—slowly and painfully."

He has the look in his eyes of hate. I know the look because I've seen it on lots of folks faces when they look at me.

"I get that, Teo. I do. And truth is, I wished them all dead a couple hundred times on the night they took me. But you know what one of the worst parts was?"

"What?" His voice is hollow now; he can't take too much more of this.

"They didn't give me a thing to eat or drink the whole time they had me. Now, I wasn't hungry, seeing as I was in a world of hurt, but shit, I got so thirsty. A tall glass of water ended up being all I could think about...and I begged for it."

Mateo nods and swallows deep, and I know at some point in his life, he begged too.

"Now it's your turn to talk, Teo. I shared my shit; time for you to share yours."

MATT

When I look at Vedie—beaten, bruised, starved, and terrorized—it's like looking at Matthew North when he was a tortured kid named Mark Blankenship, living against his will with a pedophile he had to call "Dad," and somehow dealing with it. Accepting it as simply the way things had to be. But knowing I'd shortened Vedie's stay in hell makes something inside me sing, although what I hear coming from inside me isn't so much a song as it is a battle cry—I want to go to war with everyone who hurt him.

In any case, the two of us share common experiences, and because of that, I trust him. I know he won't hold me in his mind as forever the victim, but instead, he'll see I'm a survivor. And all in all, I may not be a pretty picture—my scars paint a vivid picture of what I endured—but I did survive.

"I've lived alone for the past ten years because I needed to heal."

Vedie slinks across the towel so he's close beside me and leans his head against my shoulder, his tangle of loose dreads poking at my cheek and ear. He must know it'll be easier for me to speak, to tell him the disturbing story of my life, if we're not staring into each other's eyes.

"I needed to be alone because everything was taken from me once. I thought I was too smart to put myself in the position to lose it all again." Vedie stays quiet, so I go on. "I thought I'd be safe, all alone here on an island—far from family and friends and all reminders of what had been stolen from me when I was seven. And for a long time, I was safe. But when you came into my life, I wanted more."

I breathe and swallow deeply, waiting to see if he has anything to say, but he doesn't.

"Daniel Blankenship grabbed me from my brand-new birthday bike, a BMX like yours..."

"But without a hot-pink seat?" Vedie asks sincerely, and I smile.

"No. It didn't have a hot-pink seat." I clear my throat and continue. "I was seven when he took me, and fifteen when he brought me home."

"I'm glad he brought you home instead of, you know..." He extends one hand and gestures as if it's a gun, and shoots. "Bang, bang."

"Me too. As I got older, though, I worried all the time he'd kill me. He wasn't as interested in...you know, in me as my body got more mature, and the time finally came that he had to take me home or...or take me out. So he dropped me off down the street from my house, and then he parked in the very place he took me and blew his brains out."

I've told Vedie this before—how the man who hurt me was now dead—but still he jerks against my arm as if I've surprised him.

"I never told anybody before what I'm going to tell you now, Vedie." I pause for a few seconds, trying to decide if this is the right thing to do. But I said I'd talk, and I'm trying to be a man of my word. "Even though I feared and hated him for what he did to me, a part of me was hurt that he killed himself. That he cared so little for me after living eight years as a warped sort of father and son, he'd deprive me of seeing justice done, and of allowing me to vent my anger on the person who deserved it. But it was more than only those things..."

"I wanna know. What else?"

I sniff and force the words from my mouth. "It hurt that he could leave the world without saying goodbye to me."

Vedie's quiet for a few seconds. And then he says, "I get that, Teo, because it hurts that my brothers could mess me up me the way they did. They're supposed to love me—we grew up together, you know?"

He's relating each of my experiences to his own, which convinces me he understands me in a way no one else ever has.

"I don't enjoy talking about what went on during those eight years. But I will tell you..." I stop for a second, knowing now's the perfect time to disassociate, but again, I stay present on the sandy beach with Vedie. "I'll tell you that he raped me and beat me and manipulated me over and over, and somehow, I kept on surviving."

"You think you're weak, but you're actually real strong."

"I think you're right. And I'm getting stronger." I stop to collect my thoughts. "My parents had no idea what to do with me when I came back. And I had no clue what to do in a straight-laced family in an upscale neighborhood in a well-to-do town. 'No rules' had been my way of life, and all of a sudden, I was back to being somebody's little boy. It didn't work."

I can feel soft puffs of breath on my arm as Vedie waits for me to continue.

"And they sent me away to high school, as if I needed to be away from home any longer. But I did well, academically speaking, in boarding school, and I went right on to college and finished in three years. I've been down here working ever since. Hiding from life."

Finally Vedie looks up at me; his eyes are wider than ever, but he's not crying over the details of my disastrous youth. "Until *I* found you."

"Yes, that's right. And now, we have a chance to get some justice for you. I never had the chance to see my story end with what's fair and right, but you do, if you decide to go to the police and report the people who assaulted you."

"I'll seriously think about it." He looks out over the ocean, and the compassion on his face turns into sadness. "The thing is, Mateo, some shit about me has changed since they took me."

My honesty is rewarded. "I know."

Vedie stands up and takes a few steps toward the beach. He's far slimmer than he was a month ago—a result of physical and emotional suffering. "You noticed that *she* hasn't been around? You know, the female part of me..."

"Yes, I noticed." I stand and step up right behind him.

"I'm afraid you're not gonna want me if my girlish side doesn't come back." His voice sounds so young and scared.

"You have nothing to fear." I circle my arms around his middle and kiss him in the sensitive place between his neck and shoulder. "Can I still kiss you like this when you're feeling all the way a man?" I kiss him one more time.

He shivers. "Course you can."

"Can I hold you in bed when you're all man?"

Vedie nods. "Uh-huh."

"Can we make love to each other as soul mates— whether you're feeling your male side or your female side, or when you're at any other place that works for you?"

"Well, yeah."

"Then that's all I need. This relationship is about the love and trust we share, not about how you express your gender."

In the circle of my arms, Vedie turns around and lifts his lips to mine for a kiss, which I gladly bestow. "I sure got lucky on the day I met you, Teo."

"I don't think it's quite that simple. I think it's finally our turn for happiness. We've paid our dues. And maybe we're more complicated in some ways than other people—but now it's time to live."

Vedie lifts himself onto his toes, places his hands on my shoulders, and kisses me. It stirs me and doesn't scare me. Every aspect of us works.

We stand in the sand and kiss until the sun goes down, well concealed by the shadows of tall palm trees and dusk, but no longer hidden from each other.

MATT'S JOURNAL DATED SEPTEMBER 2015

I don't know what to make of this guy I just met at The Only Tiki Hut—a new busboy named Vedie. And I have no clue what I was thinking when I took him home last night—I wasn't even drunk. Just lonelier than usual, I guess. And something about him spoke to me.

It's sad as hell, and I admit I don't understand it, but, even though I zoned out soon after he got here and left the guy basically alone all night in my cottage, it was the best night I've had in years.

I know it can't turn into anything because of the limits I put on my life. But for a few minutes last night, I forgot I was Crazy Matt. I was just a regular guy who met somebody nice. A person who made me want more than my solitary existence.

Like that'll ever happen in this life.

Epilogue

MATT

"It's interesting."

Vedie's balancing on his toes, painting the wooden stand of our new porch swing a shade that makes me think of ripe mangoes.

"What's so interesting?" he asks. "How we're not setting up our porch swing on the porch?"

Our swing is permanently placed on the grass by the beach in the backyard. Vedie and I decided we would better enjoy the ocean view and breeze here than on the cottage's actual porch, which is more or less my gym.

"No. Putting it on the edge of the beach makes complete sense."

"What's interesting, then, Teo?" After putting his paintbrush in the can, he sits beside me on the swing. "I'm all ears."

Seeing his bright eyes and windblown hair and the smile that never seems to quit these days, I have to disagree. "From where I'm sitting, Vedie, you look like a lot more than just ears." I look him up and down. "Much more."

As I guessed, he tears up and sniffs in an effort to keep his composure. Lately, he wears his feelings on his sleeves more often than not.

"When I was young, way back before Daniel took me, I thought normal meant I'd spend the rest of my childhood swimming and skiing and riding my bike."

"That's sweet, but it's not real interesting."

I send him a wink and continue, "I also figured I'd study hard and play sports in high school, go to an Ivy League college, and then Yale Law School, the way my dad did."

"You thought all that stuff when you were only six years old?" He pulls his loose dreads up into a bun right on the top of his head and fastens it with the elastic waiting on his wrist. "When I was six, I was just trying to figure out how I could get my hands on Mama's magenta lipstick."

I laugh, picturing a miniature version of Vedie dreaming up ways to get his greedy hands into his mother's makeup bag. "In my family, the kids all knew from birth that we were destined for an Ivy League college and Yale Law. So we were prepared at a young age to study hard."

"Well, that *is* interesting." He crosses his legs and leans against me.

"That isn't the interesting part."

Vedie looks up at me and smiles. "Oh, good, because I was hoping to be more floored by whatever you thought was so amazing."

I laugh again. "The interesting part, Vedie, is I found a whole new way of being normal."

"What do you mean?"

"I found a new normal. And you found it too."

He wrinkles his forehead, not following my logic.

"It took a few weeks after you got back from being trapped at the motel with your brothers to feel safe enough, but you finally let yourself feel feminine again, right?" Vedie nods slowly. "And you're living with me here—we're partners now. When you were a kid, did you ever expect this to be your adult life? Because I'll tell you this much—when I was young and thought of being a 'normal' adult, it certainly wasn't this."

"But you like this new normal, don't you?" he asks quickly.

"Don't worry; it's perfect, just not what I expected. And I think it's because recovery from what happened to us doesn't happen in a straight line." He slides his face down my chest, so his head is in my lap. When he looks up at me expectantly, I know he wants me to explain. "Seems to me, Vedie, surviving pain and fear and confusion, the way we did, isn't the same as skipping across a grassy field. It's more like climbing over rocks, then having to turn back to find a new path when the first one ends at a cliff and falling down hard and skinning our knees on a root and bleeding. And maybe not ending up at the top of the hill, as we thought we would, but finding happiness somewhere along the way."

His eyes get wide. "I think I feel yah."

I find myself laughing yet again, and because he makes me laugh so easily and often, I practically bend in half to kiss him. Laughter wasn't part of my life until Vedie came along.

"It took us both a lot of time to get to new normal, huh, Teo?"

"It did."

"You had to live alone for a hell of a long time to get to your new normal, and I had to get beat on for years before I went to the cops and told them who was hurting me so I could find mine."

"We don't have to stay victims, you know."

"I'm smart—I've already figured that out." He stands up and pulls off the oversized white T-shirt I let him borrow on one of our first days together that he never gave back. He's naked beneath it. "But you helped me believe it when you accepted me for me."

"No bathing suit today?"

"I'm feeling in the middle right now." In the middle is Vedie's way of saying he isn't willing to commit to feeling particularly feminine or masculine. And when he's feeling this way, he wants to be naked. Another part of our new normal—one that makes me glad I have a private beach.

"I have no complaints." I strip off my shorts. "And I can meet you in the middle—it's not a problem." Who in his right mind would complain about a man as beautiful as Vedie running around naked in his backyard?

"You can meet me if you can catch me."

I watch for a few seconds as Vedie—slim and brown and lithe—darts off toward the surf. Just as I do, he has physical scars—the ones on his thighs are easy to see, as well as the new mark beneath his eye. And he can see the ones on my back. We both have emotional scars, too. By mutual agreement, we now look at our lives in terms of "before" and "after" the painful events occurred, but we're much more than merely the sum of what happened to us.

Like Vedie, I blink away the wetness in my eyes, because now isn't the time for tears, and then I sprint down the beach toward the most important part of my future, splashing naked in the waves.

About the Author

Mia Kerick is the mother of four exceptional children—one in law school, another a professional dancer, a third studying at Mia's alma mater, Boston College, and her lone son finally off to college. (Yes, the nest is empty.) She has published more than twenty books of LGBTQ romance when not editing National Honor Society essays, offering opinions on college and law school applications, helping to create dance bios, and reviewing scholarship essays. Her husband of twenty-five years has been told by many that he has the patience of Job, but don't ask Mia about this, as it's a sensitive subject.

Mia focuses her stories on the emotional growth of troubled people in complex relationships. She has a great affinity for the tortured hero in literature, and as a teen, Mia filled spiral-bound notebooks with tales of tortured heroes and stuffed them under her mattress for safekeeping. She is thankful to NineStar Press for providing her with an alternate place to stash her stories.

Her books have been featured in Kirkus Reviews magazine and have won Rainbow Awards for Best Transgender Contemporary Romance and Best YA Lesbian Fiction, a Reader Views' Book by Book Publicity Literary Award, the Jack Eadon Award for Best Book in Contemporary Drama, an Indie Fab Award, a Royal Dragonfly Award for Cultural Diversity, and a Story Monsters Purple Dragonfly Award for YA Fiction, among other awards.

Mia Kerick is a social liberal and cheers for each and every victory made in the name of human rights. Her only major regret: never having taken typing or computer class in school, destining her to a life consumed with two-fingered pecking and constant prayer to the Gods of Technology. Contact Mia at miakerick@gmail.com or visit at www.miakerickya.com to see what is going on in Mia's world.

Email: miakerick@gmail.com

Facebook: www.facebook.com/mia.kerick

Twitter: @MiaKerick

Website: www.miakerickya.com

Instagram: @Mia_Kerick_author

Other books by this author

Love Spell
The Art of Hero Worship

Coming Soon from Mia Kerick

The Scarecrow and George C.

Blurb

High school senior Van Liss is barely human. He thinks of himself as a scarecrow—ragged and unnerving, stuck and destined to spend his life cold and alone. If he ever had feelings, they were stomped out long ago by his selfish mother and her lecherous boyfriend. All he's been left with is bitter contempt, to which he clings.

With a rough exterior long used to keep the world at bay, Van spooks George Curaco, the handsome new fry cook at the diner where he works. But George C senses there is more to the untouchable Van and refuses to stop staring, fascinated by his eccentricity. When Van learns that George C is even more cold, alone, and frightened than himself, Van welcomes him to his empty home. And ends up finding his heart.

Their road to trust is rocky and, at times, even dangerous. And looming evil threatens to keep them apart forever.

Fair warning: You may want to strap in. It's going to be a bumpy ride.

Also Available from NineStar Press

Connect with NineStar Press

Website: NineStarPress.com

Facebook: NineStarPress

Facebook Reader Group: NineStarNiche

Twitter: @ninestarpress

Tumblr: NineStarPress

www.ingramcontent.com/pod-product-compliance
Lightning Source LLC
Chambersburg PA
CBHW032125180726
48284CB00002B/696